L.V.

D0323520

4

WITHDRAWN

 Usurpers

863.6
Aylu

USURPERS

 Francisco Ayala

Translated by Carolyn Richmond

Schocken Books NEW YORK

First published by Schocken Books 1987

10 9 8 7 6 5 4 3 2 1   87 88 89 90

English translation copyright © 1987 by Schocken Books Inc.
Originally published in Spanish as *Los usurpadores* by
Editorial Sudamericana; copyright © 1949, 1969, 1978
by Francisco Ayala
All rights reserved

Library of Congress Cataloging in Publication Data
Ayala, Francisco, 1906–
Usurpers.
Translation of: Los usurpadores.
1. Spain—History—Fiction. I. Title.
PQ6601.Y3U713 1987   863'.62   84–23602

Design by Jane Byers Bierhorst
Manufactured in the United States of America
ISBN 0-8052-3970-7

Contents

CAT Mar14'88

2-8-88 Coutts 12.76

ALLEGHENY COLLEGE LIBRARY

87-5157

Translator's Introduction

Francisco Ayala is without a doubt one of the great masters of Spanish prose. Born in the Andalusian city of Granada in 1906, he is the author of four novels, nine volumes of short fiction, and countless books of social and literary criticism. Recently the first two volumes of his memoirs, for which he was awarded the National Prize for Literature in 1983, have been delighting Spanish readers. His unique contribution to the world of letters and ideas has long been recognized by both the general public and critics at home and abroad. As a writer of fiction, Ayala has frequently been described as a "classic in his own lifetime." Today, as an essayist and prophet in his own land after many years of exile, he addresses the conscience of his nation.

Ayala did not always enjoy such a satisfactory relationship with the Spanish reading public, which was denied all access to his works for several decades after the end of the Civil War in 1939. At that time, the author, who had served the Spanish Republic in a number of ways (he was Secretary to its legation in Prague), was forced into exile. He had already earned himself a position of respect in the Spanish literary world, having published two novels, a volume of vanguard short stories, and a number of essays about that new and influential art form of the period: the cinema. In 1929, as a scholarship student in Germany, he was to witness at first hand the rise of

Nazism. In 1934, he was awarded a professorship at the University of Madrid.

When the Civil War broke out in 1936, Ayala returned from a lecture tour in South America to work for his country's democratically elected government. He would go back to the New World at the conclusion of that bloody conflict to make his home for the next decade in Buenos Aires, where, along with several books of essays, many on political science, and his monumental *Treatise on Sociology*, he also published, in 1949, two complementary yet independent volumes of short fiction, *The Lamb's Head* and *Usurpers*, which refer, either directly or indirectly, to those passionate and violent events of war that the author had experienced from the very eye of the storm.

The fact that these two books appeared in the same year suggests that Ayala wrote them simultaneously. Actually, they were composed successively: with the exception of a later addition, the contents of *Usurpers*—a volume of tales based, with varying degrees of fidelity, on historical moments in the Spanish past—antedate the stories of *The Lamb's Head*, which are all centered around the Civil War itself. Indeed, *Usurpers* seems almost to have liberated—even exorcised—the author to be able to write about that national tragedy which turned out to be the prelude to World War II. It is significant that, after a narrative silence of ten years, during which time he dedicated himself to the essay, Ayala's first work of fiction was a moving prose poem entitled "Dialogue of the Dead: A Spanish Elegy," published in Buenos Aires in 1939 (barely a year after his father and a brother had been assassinated by the fascists), which he later incorporated into *Usurpers* as a kind of lyric epilogue that would also serve as a thematic link between this book and *The Lamb's Head*.

In 1944 Ayala published "The Bewitched," which was immediately acclaimed by Argentine critics, among them Jorge Luis Borges, and later, along with five other tales—"The Bell of Huesca" (1943), "The Embrace" (1945), "San Juan de Dios" (1946), "The Invalid"

(1946), and "The Impostors" (1947)—incorporated into the first edition of *Usurpers*. The book was prefaced by a fictional "Explication Written by a Journalist and Archivist at the Request of the Author, His Friend," which appears in this translation as an appendix. This piece, signed in such a way as to dissemble the real author's complete name—F[rancisco] de Paula A[yala] G. Duarte—is a pseudo-pedantic tour de force that managed to deceive many people at the time, including more than one professional commentator. An expanded edition of *Usurpers* (1969) also included the following postscript, signed by "F. A.," at the end of the "Explication": "In 1950, after publishing the volume of *Usurpers*, I wrote still one more tale, 'The Inquisitor,' belonging to the same vein, which I had thought exhausted, but which nonetheless yielded this late fruit. It is now incorporated in the cycle where it belongs."

The history of *Usurpers* subsequent to that first edition parallels, in a sense, that of its author, who, in 1950, reluctant to continue living in Argentina under the dictatorship of Juan Perón, accepted an offer to teach at the University of Puerto Rico, thus embarking upon a distinguished career as professor of Spanish literature that would take him, eight years later, to the continental United States, where he taught at institutions such as New York University, the University of Chicago, and the City University of New York, from which he retired in 1976. Prior to 1960, when Ayala visited his country for the first time after the war, the Franco regime had virtually eliminated his name from the history of Spanish literature. While stories from *Usurpers* were being translated, anthologized, and studied in university classrooms throughout the United States, the book could only be read clandestinely in Spain. Although a volume of short fiction entitled *A Monkey's Tale* appeared in a very limited edition in Madrid in 1955, the censors prohibited publication of his magnificent pair of novels, *Dog's Death* (1958), translated into English six years later as *Death as a Way of Life*, and *The Bottom of the Glass* (1962).

In the early 1960s, which saw the entry of Spain into the United Nations, the rapid growth of that country's tourist industry, and the flowering of the Latin American novel, censorship gradually began to relax its grip, permitting a whole generation of Spanish readers to discover their own writers in exile. Although Ayala's next volume of stories, *The Ace of Clubs* (1962), had to be published in Buenos Aires, his short novel *The Abduction* (1965) was printed in Spain. Several of the tales from *Usurpers* were also collected into a volume in 1966, and *Dog's Death* was issued in paperback two years later. Ayala continued to make regular trips to his country, taking its pulse and gradually assuming a major role in its cultural life. But his intellectual prominence did not exempt him from the ubiquitous scissors of censorship: because he refused to allow the elimination of one text, as late as 1969, his *Complete Narrative Works*—which included the expanded edition of *Usurpers*—had to be published in Mexico.

The first complete edition of *Usurpers* to be published in Spain appeared in 1970, followed, in 1971, by a paperback edition that has gone through a number of printings. Meanwhile, Ayala continued to create new fictional works of a more intimate nature. With *The Garden of Delights*, originally published in Barcelona in 1971 and awarded the coveted Premio de la Crítica, he fully reestablished that long-lost harmony with readers of his native land.

Francisco Ayala's definitive return to Spain to live, in 1976, coincided with General Franco's death and the end of forty years of dictatorship. Since then, he has kept pace with the cultural life of the new constitutional monarchy, contributing influential articles and essays to major newspapers, lecturing, working on his memoirs, and continuing to write fiction. Considered something of the doyen of Spanish intellectuals, he is respected by young and old alike for his lucid and independent mind. His novels and short fiction are studied in Spanish high schools and universities. His 1984 election to the Spanish Royal Academy was widely celebrated, and he was invited to inaugurate the King Juan Carlos Chair at New York University in the spring of 1986.

Ayala's homeland may be Spain, and Spanish his language of expression, but his themes are universal. Time and again, in both his fiction and his essays, he returns to the subject of the human condition, which, he believes, has remained essentially the same since the Fall of Man. Nowhere is this better illustrated than in *Usurpers*, whose seven tales, based on different historical events of medieval and Golden Age Spain, all attest to the terrible corrupting force of power. Nor is it difficult to see in the ambition, violence, and surrender portrayed therein, in the hatred and—also—the love, a reflection, not just of that country's Civil War, but of mankind's eternal struggle for power.

That the fascination exerted by power and the consequences of this fascination are at the core of the book is explicitly stated by the author's "friend," the apocryphal and erudite Portuguese commentator invented by Ayala to "explicate" his text. Despite his initials, F. de Paula A. G. Duarte is neither a real person nor the author's alter ego. He is, instead, another imaginary character, another narrative voice (almost, but not quite, as anonymous as those of the "Dialogue of the Dead," and even more pedantic than that of "The Bewitched") in yet another piece of fiction. Thus his "Explication" should be read as a sort of fictional invention in which the real author's intellectual consciousness of the content and style of his book is disguised, artistically, in the words of the learned literary critic from Coimbra. Present-day readers should bear in mind both the historical moment and the uprooted author's personal circumstances, when, after finishing the main body of the book, they embark upon the "Explication"; they will discover there many interesting clues to the author's creative intent.

The central theme of the work is stated there as follows: "power exercised by man over his fellow man is always a usurpation." The narrator analyzes how this ideological phenomenon manifests itself in the six original narrations, which, as he says, "interrelate in different ways," and he explains both the author's choice, and careful use of historical settings, and his awareness of style. With the addition of "The Inquisitor," Ayala completed his depiction of the human passions giving rise to violence with a factor of paramount importance: fanaticism. The tale is based on a situation that occurred more than once in the history of Spain: that of the convert who, possessed with the ardor of the neophyte, relentlessly pursues his former coreligionists. This portrayal of the rigidity and intellectual arrogance of the fanatic mind has been especially popular with students of Spanish literature in the United States.

Usurpers is a work of great stylistic unity, within which there exist rhetorical differences consciously ascribed by the author to the various narrators and characters of each of the pieces. This fine, but important, distinction presents a major challenge to the translator. Ayala's sentences, frequently long and syntactically complex, unfold before our eyes with a sinuous rhythm that is at once fluid and carefully controlled: the elegant, often baroque line of his prose is, in fact, measured, even austere. He is always precise. In *Usurpers*, with its rich imagery, intensity of feeling, and intellectual complexity, no word, no phrase has been left to chance.

This is the first complete translation of *Usurpers* into English. I have had the privilege of working closely with the author, who is himself a translator, and an accomplished one at that. The characteristics of Ayala's style seemed to me to preclude from the start an overly free translation; they demanded, instead, as faithful a recreation as possible. I have tried to offer readers a mirror of the original by combining, insofar as possible, precision with poetry. I have respected the length of paragraphs and sentences, eliminated nothing, and taken special pains with the author's use of metaphor. The reader will find that certain bodily parts of characters are sometimes granted almost complete autonomy. One of the first Spaniards to write about the cinema as an art form, Ayala often takes advantage of the visual potential of language, offering us, time and again, close-ups and moving shots that emphasize the intimate relationship between a character's immediate physical reality and his or her inner being.

As the Explicator points out, these tales are based on "historical situations that are well known" to Ayala's readers. Since the English-speaking public is unlikely to have the same degree of familiarity with Spanish history and culture, I have included a limited number of brief notes of a purely informational nature, the majority of them identifications. In addition, there are a few notes intended to clarify other kinds of allusions or to explain an occasional word that has been left in the original Spanish.

CAROLYN RICHMOND

 Usurpers

San Juan de Dios

Kneeling beside the cot, the anguish of death on his face, his hands clenching the shank of a crucifix—even now I seem to see, emaciated and tinged with green, the profile of the saint. I can see it still: there in the house where I was born, on the front wall of the parlor. Though very somber, it was a fine painting with its ochers and its blacks, and its deep purples, and that harsh slash of light, so weak that it barely managed to highlight the praying image. Time has passed. A long time has passed: memorable events, unforeseen changes, and horrible experiences. But behind the thick web of pride and honor, miseries, ambitions, yearnings, behind the infamy and the hate and the forgive-and-forget, that motionless image, that mortal scene, remains fixed, clear, in the depths of my memory, with the same obscure silence that so astonished our childhood when we still knew almost nothing about that blessed Juan de Dios, a soldier of Portuguese birth, who—one afternoon in the month of June, more than four centuries ago—had arrived as a foreigner at the gates of the city where he is now venerated, to become, after many hardships, the saint whose exemplary death an unknown artist's hand wished to perpetuate for the renewed

Saint John of God (1495–1550) founded the Brothers Hospitalers, a religious institute devoted to the care of the sick, in Granada, Spain, in 1540.

3

edification of generations to come, and about whose life I am now going to write.

Over four hundred years ago, as I was saying (not long after the Moorish kingdom, divided into factions, torn apart by the endless feuding of its clans, had surrendered as a province to the Crown of the Catholic Monarchs),* this Juan de Dios, an oldish-looking and taciturn youth, lean of body, his eyelids reddened by dust from the coast, enlisted in the garrison of the fortress. At that time, animosity stemming from reciprocal offenses and family rancors had not yet yielded in Granada to the nostalgia for a recently lost magnificence. The Gomeles and Zegris had had to abandon the land; the Gazules and the noble Abencerages† had in turn recovered their possessions, receiving military commissions in the Christian companies, public posts in the city. But violence—the same violence that, years later, would gush forth from the Alpujarran peaks to scald the skin of all Spain in the cruel rebellion of the Moriscos‡—was now, its fury still smothered, snorting and

*Fernando II of Aragon (1452–1516) and Isabel I of Castile (1451–1504), whose marriage in 1469 produced the eventual unification of Spain, completed in 1492 with the fall of the kingdom of Granada.

†Four of the noble clans in the fifteenth century whose rivalry was one of the causes of the fall of that Moorish kingdom. Zoraya, a Spaniard who had converted to Islam and was the new favorite of Sultan Mulay Abu Hassan (1462–85), had borne him a son. Aixa, the discarded favorite, fearing that her own son, Boabdil, might be disinherited, fled with him to Guadix, where he was proclaimed king. Boabdil, who had contrived to dethrone his father, was taken prisoner by the Spaniards at Lucena in 1483 and set free only after swearing allegiance to King Fernando. Although Boabdil's power was restored, he was eventually forced to relinquish Granada to the Catholic Monarchs in 1492. The Gomeles and Zegris supported Aixa and Boabdil; the Gazules and Abencerages were supporters of Zoraya.

‡The revolt of the Moriscos (Christianized Moors) in the Alpujarra mountains around Granada in 1568–71 was savagely repressed by Don Juan de Austria (see p. 73n), whose troops laid waste the surrounding countryside.

snarling in all corners. To the anger of the old factions was added a suspicious hatred and dread of the intruders who had arrived with the new rule. So daybreak each morning saw the streets and famous squares of Granada and the banks of the river littered with corpses vomited up by the turbid night.

In the midst of those civil divisions that add hypocrisy to hatred and treason to ferocity, our Juan de Dios discovered his calling as a saint. He found it—what was he, poor man, but a simple soldier?—through the learned, ardent, and florid words of that virtuous and illustrious man Juan de Avila,* later beatified by the Church, who, seconding Their Majesties' Christian policy, was at that time preaching the Gospel to the Granadans, with invectives, apostrophes, and threats that crackled like grains of salt spilled out upon so much fire. The fervor of one of his sermons, it seems, was what made Juan abandon the profession of arms, distribute his belongings among the poor, and, having acquired the riches of poverty, devote his life to relieving the sufferings of others.

They say that in so doing he obeyed a sudden impulse: the preacher's voice, which he had so often heard unheedingly, this time pierced his eardrums and scalded his bosom, invading him with sudden fright. He was—they say—lost there among the faithful, withdrawn, huddled up, his mind wandering, when suddenly he felt himself assaulted by a strange certainty, so strange, in truth, that he took a good while before surrendering to it: the certainty that the Holy Spirit in person was addressing his forgotten insignificance, and that the pathetic tremolos of its voice were rebuking him, him in particular, Juan, from the preacher's pulpit. According to what one of his disciples—later bent upon coaxing from the saint's reluctant lips some detail of that revelation—left in writing, we

*Spanish preacher and ascetic prose writer (1500–1569) who dedicated much of his life to missionizing the towns of Andalusia.

know how his heart jumped within his breast when he realized—these were his very words—that he was *exposed*. It was,
it seems, a sort of startled awakening. He awoke, indeed,
there, in that shadowy corner, at the foot of the column,
beneath the padre's accusing finger. Then he tried to pay
attention and he was scarcely able, at the start, to make out
the meaning of his thunderous phrases; but he felt, unavoid-
ably, that stiff finger aimed straight at him, at him, precisely
at him, as he knelt there among so many others, pointing
him out in the middle of the flock, distinguishing him, despite
his attempt to dissemble, feign innocence, and pretend to
know nothing: ready to hook him, to draw him up from the
ground, to heave him in the air, and—suspending him in the
midst of that milky light which crossed the transept of the
church from above—to expose him to their scorn as a repro-
bate, the implacable finger came back time and again, irritated, furious, enraged, to his sad insignificance.

Juan bowed his head and, with it lowered, could now catch
something, some flashing phrase or so, from the flood of the
preacher's words. "I'm talking to you," he cried out, "to you,
Old Christian, * who have succumbed. . . ." Juan de Dios, an
Old Christian from the realm of Portugal, had succumbed,
and he was plunging down that craggy precipice along which
each new step leads toward the dark abyss. Through the gates
of the flesh, mortal sin had entered his soul. And thus, abandoned body and soul to the delights of Moorish customs,
clinging like an unclean cur to the enemies of the Faith, his
criminal friendship had made him hear in silence, from their
venomous and honeyed mouths, jibes directed against Our
Lord and His Church. Rather than coming out in defense of
the true God—he would have been ashamed to acknowledge

* A descendant of Christians with no known trace of Moorish or Jewish
blood.

Him—he had heard their infamies meekly, with false, cowardly smiles. And how long had he lived in such abjection, wallowing among the fetid flowers of that marsh? "Ah, what a long, horrible, deceptive dream! Many are those who die in their sleep. Awake! You there, Christian, awake!"

Afterward Juan de Dios approached to ask for confession, and Juan de Avila, seeing tears of anguish in his eyes, agreed to hear his sins. "For years and years I've lived with a viper hidden in my bosom, and not till today did I awake to mortal sin. My father, your cry awakens me. Save me from sin! Confession, father!"

"My son, expel that viper at once; speak, confess. What sins do you acknowledge?" was his answer. Then Juan began to confess. He declared his carnal sin. And then he also imputed to himself blasphemies to which his cowardice had made him tacitly assent: he had listened to, he had agreed to, he had joined in the laughter. Was he not an apostate, then? the soldier asked, bursting into tears. And although the confessor drew distinctions and granted him absolution without a serious penance, Juan did not feel himself relieved, nor did he think himself cleansed. An insatiable desire for confession took hold of him from that moment; he wanted to make a public confession; he wanted to proclaim the abomination of his sins, shout his crime to the rooftops, declare himself a betrayer of Christ, and feel over his head the horror, the pity, and—if possible, the forgiveness of the entire world.

He divested himself of his meager possessions and, after much sorrow and anguish, one Sunday, during high mass, he raised his voice in the collegiate church. As he knelt in the center of the nave, his arms in the form of a cross seemed to bear with enormous effort the burden of his sins. And the faithful, drawn from their devotions by that harsh voice accusing itself without respite, stared at the penitent, more taken by surprise than edified: amid the splendor of their gold and brocades, his rags; in the midst of such dignified composure, his shaven head, his parched throat, his imploring hands. Bewildered, they gazed at him, almost scandalized. But he went on confessing his sins: he scourged his frailty, he pounded his face with his fists, he clawed his chest. How far would he go in his frenzy? Now he acknowledged having disparaged God by idolizing human creatures; he acknowledged that, driven by that idolatry to the ultimate frailty of reason, he had gone so far as to doubt the Most Holy Trinity. His lamentations increased and, along with them, the gravity of the sins proclaimed and the stupefaction of the faithful. Until, at last, after much hesitation and not without some commotion, a deacon and two acolytes went over to him and firmly asked that he leave the church, for—as they explained to him—his public penance was more likely to inspire scorn than piety.

But how could the wretched man have restrained his heart's abundance? A week later he appeared in the middle of the Puerta Real,* shouting before the multitude the pain of his infamy. In the midst of a dense crowd, he beat his breast and wept: he had committed apostasy, abjuring the true religion to follow that of the false prophet! The people who had gathered around to listen soon passed from curiosity to derision, and they began to feed his excitement with malicious questions. And after that day he was often found exposing his afflictions in any of the city's public places: in the market, in some small square, and even before the Episcopal Palace itself. Finally, he was seized and interned in an insane asylum.

But his mildness would soon burst his chains, and his resignation would not be long in breaking the bars of the madhouse: he made of the prison a school of charity. And when

*A center of activity in Granada, located where the Royal Gate once stood.

they unlocked its doors for him, he no longer had any goal in the world other than to found a hospital for the poor. To this work he was to consecrate the remainder of his life.

The episode in that holy life that this story proposes to bring to light had its beginnings one summer morning when Juan de Dios had gone out, as was his wont, to walk through the streets begging charitable assistance. It was close to the silent, deserted, hot noon hour. Through the Zacatín,* at whose entrance he was stationed, he heard a horse approach, striking with its collected gait the cobblestones of the street. The blessed beggar went forth to meet it and, taking hold of the bridle, entreated its rider with his habitual litany: "My lord, succor the poor in Christ Jesus. Alms for ——" But the rider, jerking at the reins, raised his whip and struck the beggar's shaven head. "Alms, my lord, for the love of God," repeated Juan, who had fallen at the feet of the bristling beast. In a fit of rage, the rider raised himself high in his stirrups, bent over, and, leaning forward, flailed the beggar again and again until his face was crisscrossed with bloody furrows. Juan covered his eyes with his hands, shielded his temples and ears with his elbows, waiting for the fury to subside; he thought, on seeing the rider's boot tense in the stirrup: *I frightened him; he was taken unawares.* He thought: *Soon, soon he'll stop abusing me . . .* And before he had finished thinking it, once again he heard the horse's iron shoes striking the stones as they moved off down the street.

Juan de Dios picked up his sack, put on a sandal that had slipped from his heel, and, wiping his forehead with his sleeve, began to walk slowly, hugging the walls, toward the lane, in search of clean water with which to bathe his wounds. Beyond the last houses the stream joined the road before

*A busy Granada thoroughfare whose entrance is located at the southeast corner of Bibarrambla Square.

receding again, still following along its border, out into the countryside. There Juan stopped to rest, in the spot where the lane opened onto a dungheap; down below the pile of dung, ablaze with the sparkle of insects, trailed the water, quiet, crystal-clear, and cool. Seated on a stone, the wretched man was momentarily distracted from the pain of his bruises by the sight of a boy who, stiffened against the stubbornness of a donkey, was sweating to get him out of the dunghill in the sultry atmosphere of the summer noon. "That pitiful animal," the beggar thought as he watched the silent struggle, "must have fallen year by year into poorer and harsher hands, until, totally useless, he was finally abandoned there in the waste, without a harness, without a halter. And there he is now, forgotten by death, his head lowered, his legs dried up, his belly swollen, while the flies, persistent and cruel on his sores, suck his old blood. You are safe, tiny sky-blue flowers growing near the water, safe to smile at one another with the playfulness of little girls, within reach of his reluctant muzzle. And you, savage boy, you're flogging his backbone in vain. Nothing can make him take another step." From the depths of these reflections, he raised his voice to persuade him:

"Don't you see that he can't even move? Why don't you let him alone, boy?"

"He will, God damn it!" his rage responded, as another blow fell upon the emaciated animal's loins.

Juan did not reply. He saw the boy move back several steps, seize a stone, and hurl it at the ribs of the motionless beast.

"You see he can't move, child," he now insisted.

"But I want to take him away with me . . ."

"Whatever for?"

"Just to take him away with me."

"Stop that, child. Leave him there, and for mercy's sake come give me a little help."

Abandoning his efforts with relief, the boy now looked at the speaker for the first time, and found a face soiled with blood and dust.

"What happened, good sir?" he asked with a start.

"Only God is good. Come on. Hurry. Over here. Dip this rag in water and cleanse my head."

The boy obeyed. He went down to the stream, soaked in its current the cloth that Juan had held out to him, and returned with it dripping to sponge his brow. The wounded man clenched his teeth; it stung.

"Gently, my son; with care. Tell me, what are you called?"

"Antón."

"Gently, Antoñico."

At this moment, far down the road, in a cloud of dust and as though suspended in the hot air, they saw a coach appear, advancing and growing larger in the solitary countryside. Both of them, man and boy, stared fixedly at its remoteness; with the jingling of the mules, everything became larger and acquired volume before them in the dense atmosphere, everything gradually took on its natural size. The coach came up at last to where they were standing and slowed down at the bend; but, instead of picking up speed again, it came to a halt a little farther on. What was it the coachman, from atop his box, was shouting at them now?—He was asking them at his mistress' bidding if they had had an accident.

The holy beggar then ran up to the coach to beg for alms. "For the love of God, my lady!" he implored with his hand held out. But the anticipated coins did not fall into it; instead, the softest of words tinkled in his ear: "How did you get that wound?" and his eyes turned at once toward the sound. They found, indeed, something to marvel at: in the frame of the window was seen, adorned with garnets and pearls, a head whose beauty was the faithful reflection of a loving heart.

"It's nothing, God knows. It's not worth my worrying about, let alone my lady's attention," replied the beggar. "This boy has bathed the wound for me," he added, pointing to Antón, who was straggling behind him, "and now I must go on begging for the relief of my sick. Will my lady succor them?"

"I will, indeed. But who are the sick of whom you speak, and what succor do they need?" asked the lady with renewed interest.

"Ah, madam! They are the sick nobody thinks of caring for, because they have no kindred but their maladies and their poverty. These I shelter and care for in the house where, along with their afflictions, I hope to heal my soul. Some gentlefolk who know of my work and are in a position to help, lend me daily assistance. And those who, passing by, are moved by my appeal, make up the rest."

"I wish to be one of the former, my friend, not one of the passersby. Send me this lad every day, and every day I'll send something back with him for your sick."

"The lad does not belong to me, my lady. I found him wandering right here. He has done me the kindness I spoke of before, and when your ladyship happened to pass by I was just thinking about whether I ought to take him along with me. But——"

"In that case," she interrupted, "*I* must be the one who takes him into my household, if it suits him to be my page. That way I shall be able to send him to you with my daily alms, while he grows into a man in my house."

"Did you hear that, boy? Why haven't you run to kiss the lady's hand?"

Antoñico kissed the gentlewoman's fingers, so slender that the weight of her rings seemed to overwhelm them, and full of joyous haste he climbed up next to the coachman, while

engraving on his mind the hospital's address, carefully commended to his memory by Juan de Dios. A moment later, the
saint was alone: the coach had vanished in a cloud of dust;
and when he looked about him, even the poor old donkey had
vanished from the dungheap.

It took the appearance of the boy who—jubilant and
dressed in new clothes—knocked the next day at his door,
bringing him a pair of hens in his mistress' name, to prove to
him that it had all not been a dream, like others that at
times had befuddled his mind. No; there was Antoñico, self-
important and magnanimous. And the next day he would
come again, and he would keep on coming week after week,
month after month, with the testimony, ever renewed, of a
noble and remote existence.

"Look, Juan. Do you see? My hand will never scourge you
again."

Juan raised his troubled eyes from the ground. He had gone
outside to breathe: leaning against the doorjamb, he offered to
the fresh air of the patio his pallid cheeks, fatigued from the
insidious vapor that impregnated everything within, sheets,
mats, vessels, clothing, and hands. At that moment, when,
almost in a faint, he was trying to recover, he was drawn from
his confused torpor by the unexpected summons of this
wretched cripple who, presenting to him the still reddish
stumps of two recently amputated hands, said with angry,
bitter, proud, forsaken emphasis:

"Do you see, Juan? They will scourge you no more."

Juan looked at him, aghast.

"How did you lose your hands, man?"

"I lost them by way of my pride. And now, heavy-hearted,
I've come here to beg your forgiveness."

While he was speaking, Juan de Dios had been scrutinizing

the newcomer's face: a sharp, nervous, changing face, whose burning eyes filled with tears as his fine mouth spoke the last words.

"I don't know you, and I have nothing to forgive you. You must be the one to forgive *me*, if I see you in distress and cannot console you. Come in, brother. Come have a little wine with me, and tell me about your troubles."

The man followed him, with bowed head, to the kitchen, where they sat down together at a small wooden table on which there was a jug of wine.

"You must raise the glass to my lips, Juan de Dios, or I'll have to drink as animals do, for I've not yet learned to master my disability."

The cripple drank, and when his spirit had grown calm, he told the story of his misfortune, explaining how, by a terrible design of Providence, he had fallen into the trap that he himself, with such meticulous care, had set for someone else.

"My name," he began by saying, "is Don Felipe Amor. I come from an ancient Granadan family that, because of the age-old contentions of this realm, crossed over into Christian lands and settled in Lucena, where I was born. If only I'd never left! If only I'd never returned to this, my ancestral home! But I did, propelled by the two wings of ambition and of pride. Pride, because I would not resign myself to the loss of fortune that bad luck or bad judgment had inflicted on my house, even though ample remained to support an honorable and decent life. Ambition, because I was determined to reclaim from my Granadan kinsfolk the many possessions they had seized long ago, when my family was forced to abandon the land. My mind bent on this idea, I stopped at nothing. And even the defects of my education—my upbringing as a nobleman's son, whose every wish is granted, nay anticipated; the scorn I felt toward my fellow creatures; my disregard for my neighbor and sole regard for my own purposes—helped me to succeed in my intent. Today I would be rich and powerful, and respected as such despite my arrogance, abuses, and cruelties, had the hardness of my heart not been stormed and vanquished by its only vulnerable part. What I mean is that, in the course of my achievements, and having at last succeeded in recovering my family's former possessions, I still wished to round off my own fortune with that of a noble heiress whom the eldest of my cousins had been courting, and of whose qualities I had had news from his own lips. So, not content with having deprived this kinsman of mine, Don Fernando Amor, of a part of his fortune, I decided to deprive him of his lady as well. And this was carried out with such good—that is to say, with such bad—fortune for me, that destiny seemed to delight in smoothing and carpeting with flowers the paths along which I traveled, unawares, toward my doom. What Fernando had been unable to attain in years of courting, I attained in days. In less than a fortnight from the time I first met my Doña Elvira, she and I had become secretly betrothed. That fortnight saw very profound changes in the spirits of all three. Of *her* feelings I shall not speak, for what under other circumstances would have been for me a reason for justified vanity, is now one for most bitter grief. As for myself, suffice it to say that a courtship and wedding conceived in ambitious calculation were transformed by Doña Elvira's presence into so frantic a passion that I would have sacrificed in a moment, were it necessary, all the riches I had won with such arduous tenacity in long-drawn-out lawsuits. For his part, my cousin Don Fernando, who—his animosity scarcely concealed beneath his courtly manners—had already seen himself stripped of possessions he looked upon as his inheritance from his father, could not bear that on top of that humiliation there should fall this other, truly insufferable one:

ALLEGHENY COLLEGE LIBRARY

the lady he had courted preferring me in marriage. And thus, when I told him the news whose effect I had been savoring in advance, I caught a glimpse of his burning rancor in the way he looked when he congratulated me on my new fortune. He acted effusive and pleased, but in the closeness of our embrace I saw a cruel gleam in his eye. He was by nature devious and ill-tempered, and that rancor must have disturbed his judgment. Mad with spite, he committed an act unworthy of the gentle manners he tried so to affect, an act in which his fondness for Doña Elvira would combine in the vilest way with his desire to affront me. The fact is that, leaping through her window when the lady was trying on a gown for the celebration of our betrothal,* he embraced her from behind, crossing his arms over her bosom, squeezing her breasts with his hands, while her maidservants, taken aback, dumbfounded, dared not move. He fled at once from where he had come.

"No sooner had I learned of this—such troubles never want for messengers—than I began to think of some punishment equal to the crime, and I finally decided that none would be more fitting than to cut off his bold hands and to make a gift of them to Doña Elvira on the day of our betrothal. That idea alone would satisfy me. Resolved at last to set about it, I chose the time and arranged things in the best possible manner. I learned that, to keep away from the family celebration, Don Fernando planned to withdraw on the day of the festivities to an estate that still belongs to him in the lowlands of Granada, beyond the village of Maracena. Bribing one of his servants, I stationed several of mine on the road, and everything was in place for my revenge to be carried out. That was, as I said, the very day of our betrothal; and along with the executors of my

* In the past, a formal ceremony of betrothal preceded the actual wedding, sometimes by years.

punishment, there awaited an emissary who was to deliver to my bride-to-be, in a casket of wrought silver, like freshly harvested fruits, the infamous hands that had offended her modesty.

"So the celebration began, and all the while it was going on, I was anxiously awaiting the arrival of the terrible gift. I could attend to nothing. I was full of anxiety, and even the words of my bride were incapable of forcing their way into my ear, intent as it was upon the noises of the street. Finally, Doña Elvira asked me what was making me so uneasy, and I, wishing to allay her concern without betraying my own, by then far too visible, replied that I was waiting to make her a present worthy of her and of myself, and that I was feeling impatient because of the delay.

" 'But aren't the presents that you've already given me enough? What other thing do you wish to give me, and what does it matter if it arrives on time or is late?' she inquired, no doubt alarmed by my obscure reply.

" 'It matters,' I answered, 'for without that gift I shall not think myself an equal in your eyes, nor sufficiently honored on this occasion.' Imprudent words, which I don't know why I couldn't contain! And once I'd begun, yet more: 'Haven't you noticed,' I added, 'that one of my kinsmen is not among the guests?'

"On hearing this, Doña Elvira turned pale for fear of what she knew not. She took my hands and, half pleading, half threatening, she urged, 'Come, Felipe, tell me what this means. Tell me! I must know what this means.'

"I tried to evade the issue by laughing. But she besieged and pressed me so vehemently that, no longer able to resist, I yielded and told her what I had contrived, and what vengeance I'd prepared to restore my honor.

"I would have liked the earth to open and swallow me up

when I saw all her beauty was now an expression of horror. Only then did I understand that the loathsome gift must never reach her. With bloodless lips, and in a tone of severity I would never have imagined issuing from her throat, she said to me, 'I swear, Don Felipe, that if these plans are carried out I shall never be your wife.' And then, anxiously, she added, 'Hurry, hurry, for God's sake, to prevent this infamy.'

"I left the festivities, jumped on my horse, and at a full gallop raced to the spot where I had stationed my servants, hoping now that my cousin had not yet arrived so that I could countermand the order. But just as I was reining in, they emerged from the shadows to intercept me, seized hold of me, and, covering my head with a cloth, grasped my wrists. In a moment my hands had fallen, reaped by their scimitars. In the midst of the frightful confusion and the pain, I could still make out the galloping of the horse belonging to my emissary who was taking to my bride, in a silver box, not Don Fernando's hands, but my own, with the betrothal ring on one finger."

He paused for a long while. Then he concluded:

"That, Juan de Dios, is the story of my misfortune. For many days I've been turning the designs of destiny over in my mind, without being able to explain why the hands of the bridegroom had to fall, instead of the treacherous and lascivious hands of the offender. My brain was blinded by desperation. I could not understand what today I understand with absolute clarity: that it was I who was, and always have been, the true criminal, that I have been so against my own self, that it was *I* who ordered that my own hands be cut off. And now I see clearly what is my duty and the only way to purification left for me. I must kneel before Fernando and beg him to forgive me. But . . . I cannot do it! I still cannot! I've approached his door a hundred times and retreated a hundred more. I shall have to make a detour, perhaps a very long one, the longer the better. I shall have to be forgiven first by all the others whom I have offended or done violence to. That's why I'm asking for your forgiveness, Juan. Do you remember the rider who—some time ago: longer, no doubt, by the reckoning of my misfortunes than by that of the calendar—struck you when you begged alms from him in the Zacatín? It is the same man who humbles himself at your feet today."

"Rejoice, brother, and give thanks unto God, whose terrible surgery has amputated your limbs so as to save your life!"

That was Juan's exhortation when he had heard to the finish the amazing story of Don Felipe Amor.

"Rejoice!"

Then he gave him heart:

"What is it that stops you, now that your soul has seen the light, from following the righteous path? Tell me, who is leading you astray toward false and illusory byways? What insidious voice is trying to dissuade you, to put you off, to gain time for your perdition? Do what you mean to do without delay! You think you've come to ask for my forgiveness. Is it not my help you want? I think it is. But neither I nor anyone can give you help. I'll give you my company. I'll certainly give you my company. Let us go, brother; let us go together to Don Fernando's door and wait there until he goes in or comes out. When you see him, just step forward and ask his forgiveness."

So they went to do it. Don Felipe Amor had to spend a whole day waiting, while Juan de Dios was begging alms, before his cousin's house. And when that gentleman at last appeared at the door and began walking absentmindedly down the street, his way was blocked by the sudden surprise of a kneeling body, a pair of outstretched stumps, and some flustered words: "Stop, Fernando! Don't you recognize me? It's me, Felipe Amor. Yes, it's me! Are you speechless with surprise? It's me. Here I am, crippled and in rags. I need not explain—you know everything. And now, here I am, kneeling at your feet. I've come to beg your forgiveness for the harm I tried to do you and did to myself. So give me your hands, Fernando, that I may kiss them. Let me lick, like a dog, their fortunate palms."

"If I did, I'd be afraid that you'd bite them like a dog! Be off!" replied Don Fernando in a trembling voice. On recovering from his surprise, he had found himself a prisoner of wrath, choked by it. He shook himself and gave a shove to the submissive body that blocked his path, knocking it to the ground.

Then he walked away, his face pale. But on parting from his cousin, he saw between his flashes of rage the shaven head of Juan de Dios, who was running to help the fallen man. Twice more he looked back, and, about to turn the corner, he stopped, retraced his steps, and rejoined the two men, in time to wipe with his handkerchief the tears that were scalding Felipe's face.

"Wretched man!" he chided. "Couldn't you have left me in peace, after so many sorrows?" And then, in an unexpected plaintive tone: "You took from me, Felipe, all I had in the world. And now you've come to ask me for the one thing you could not have extracted from me by force: my forgiveness. Well, you're taking that too against my will! For your sake, I never would have granted it: but because of this man here I shall not deny it to you. You are forgiven!"

And leaving his cousin in the street, he drew Juan de Dios by the arm up to the entryway of his house, made him pass through the wrought-iron gate, and, once alone with him in a little room, importuned him:

"Who are you, whom I'm always running into on the path of my misfortunes? What new calamity have you come to announce to me today, lay brother of the devil? What have those bleary, cunning eyes, made to decipher riddles, read in the book of my destiny?"

"My lord, I've never seen you before. And if I know something of your misfortunes, it is not by means of secret arts," Juan replied. "I know nothing of magic, nor am I a bearer of warnings. I, Don Fernando, am a poor sinner who begs alms to maintain a hospital for——"

"Useless guile! Didn't my own ears hear the confession from that hypocritical mouth of yours? Aren't you that very fool who once shouted from the steps of the Royal Chancellery, taking upon himself all the world's crimes? All of them, including witchcraft, I'm sure. I remember clearly that I stopped a moment, but only a moment, because other cares were pressing me. Yes, I was in a hurry to learn the decision in the suit that Don Felipe had brought against me. But when I came out, my heart heavy from the ruling against me, and a bitter taste in my mouth, there you were, bellowing like a madman. You were talking—I shall never forget it!—about gold that turns to smoke, leaving one's hands and soul unclean. Why did you look at me when you said that? You knew!"

"How could I know, my lord?"

"You knew! My fortune had gone up in smoke, leaving my hands unclean from flattery and bribes, my soul unclean from cares, from rancor, from venom. . . . Nor did you know when, almost a year later, you came up to meet me on the new bridge, that I was impatient to get across so as to reach the house of Doña Elvira? You begged alms of me. You told me that time spent in giving help to the poor was not time lost. You went on and on. But I didn't listen to you. I was in a hurry that time too, a mad hurry to hear words that would seal my misfortune. And when I had received the verdict from her lips (and in so discreet a manner that it increased the value of my loss, rounding off my sorrow), I crossed the bridge again, with leaden feet, and abandoned my purse into your hands. If you knew nothing, then why did you kiss the coins without saying a word?"

"My lord, it is my wont to kiss what people give me for the love of God."

"Tell me, please, speak clearly: What warning do you bring me today? What new misfortune awaits me? Tell me once and for all."

"How could I? If my presence is a warning, someone is guiding my random steps for ends unknown to me, and which my mouth could not declare."

"I shall not part from you—do you hear!—until I know what they are. This time I will obey the call and change my course."

"Praised be the Lord! By your own tongue those ends are now declared," exclaimed Juan, filled with joy. Bursting into pious tears, he embraced the gentleman.

Don Fernando was bewildered, almost terrified, on hearing his own words resound in the air like a strange explosion, as though they were somebody else's. Had they really come out of his mouth? They had probably slipped out on impulse; he had said what he had without thinking, without calculating its scope; and only afterward was he able to gauge it, from the grave and jubilant words with which Juan de Dios had received it. There it was, in the air: it had been said. And why not? He had lost everything, and was on the way to losing his soul as well. For can a person who denies forgiveness hope to be forgiven? And he had denied it a short while before to one who had implored it of him on his knees. Still more: he had made the cripple who had asked to kiss his hands roll on the ground, when in truth it was he who should have begged forgiveness of his brother. For it was he who, by unleashing

Don Felipe's fury with the injury he had done to him on the flesh of his bride, had cut off his hands and plunged him into the depths of misery.

So he ran in search of Felipe and they were reconciled.

"Don't you see?" he said to him later, in the outpouring of their hearts. "Your arrogance and mine, the one broken against the other, had to sink into the mire, that our blood might join and truly recognize its brotherhood. Now that we are but spoils of ourselves, we reunite and we embrace. Only now do we remember that our common surname means love, not hate."

That is how both gentlemen, whose lives had been bound, mutilated, and crippled in the contrary events of a common destiny, decided to follow Juan de Dios, devoting themselves together to the office of charity, in which they hoped to uplift and save themselves. So they joined the company of the saint and assisted him unselfishly in his work, until in its harshness they had proved the mettle of their spirits, in its lowliness, their hearts' renunciation. They who had been served from birth, now served others with prompt, meek, and solicitous obedience; they whose only exercise till then had been that of chivalry, music, and pleasant games, wore themselves out in tedious, miserable chores; they who had always dressed in rich fabrics, had to defend themselves against stormy weather with rags; they whose palate and nose had been accustomed to delicate dishes and to perfumes from the Orient, had to deal with stinking pustules, lacerated and rotten flesh, excrement. Following their example, many were those who, generation after generation, disillusioned with the world, entered that new hospitaler Order; but nobody, ever, with such dedicated fervor as these two noblemen of Granada who, forgetting themselves, found no task too vile in their thirst for mortification. And in this, their backs turned to a world that was flagellating itself with such senseless rigor, they discovered a pure joy, all the more secret for being obvious and easy.

However, they still had to triumph over an occurrence so cruel that it would shake them to the deepest roots of their souls. Let us see how this blow fell upon their heads. What happened was that, for the punishment of the violent and the perfection of the pious, Heaven decided to unloose a plague upon the contumacious crimes with which Granada seethed. Its terror suddenly dissolved the animosity that years of threats and exhortations had been unable to appease; its dreadful ire annihilated the sordid grudges of irreconcilable enemies; death anticipated death, wresting from revenge its spoils; premeditated victims succumbed sooner to the pestilence than to the sword, and how often would they meet their defrauded enemies there, in the crowded heap of the common grave! Doors and windows were barred, breaths were held, in a truce of ambitions and tasks. And that handful of hospitaler brothers who, together with Juan de Dios, had vowed to alleviate the sufferings of the sick, now had to neglect them, often in dire need, so as to devote their mercy to the burial of the dead. Days and weeks went by without rest, without respite, without hope.

"How long, O Lord!" Juan de Dios had exclaimed one morning, lifting his eyes toward the indifferent blue from the dense throng of people bringing their misery to his doorstep. A great multitude had gathered their thousands of entreaties there, drawn in their need by the fame of a dedication that, being indefatigable, had come to be called miraculous. "How long, O Lord!" was his prayer. And when he lowered his eyes and again cast his gaze over those unfortunate people who were vying for the help and the consolation of a blessing from the saint, he saw among the crowd, struggling to make his way forward, arms outstretched and shouting something that could not be heard in the supplicants' clamor, that boy, Antón, who after having helped him to care for a wound, had for some time been the bearer of alms sent by his mistress to the hospital. How long had it been since he had ceased to come with the gift of her offerings and of his cheerful smile? Hadn't the last time been when he brought a splendid present, offered by her on the eve of her betrothal? After that, he had disappeared. How long had it been since then? And, how his appearance had changed!—no, no, it couldn't have been so long ago—how he had changed since then! Now too he was extending his hands; not with offerings, however, but looking gaunt, needy, and sad. Taking him by the hands, Juan de Dios led him inside to listen to his troubles. What had become of him? And what did he want, what did he need? He urged him to speak.

But the boy had only one thing to say. Grief-stricken, he cried out: "My lady, Juan! She's dying!"

He drank some water, and at last he became a bit calmer. Then he told how the sickness had entered his mistress' house and, after preying upon several of the servants, so as to make rich and poor equal, it also attacked the old master, whose defenses soon gave out.

"Once my lord was dead, all the servants fled in terror; to save their lives, they threw their gratitude overboard. And now, Juan, now it's she, Doña Elvira, my mistress, who's on the verge of death. While her father still had breath in him, his daughter remained on her feet. But now . . . And what can I do, all alone? Help me, Juan! Hurry, come with me!"

"But wait a moment. Listen. Tell me, is there none of her family left? And her husband?"

"What husband, God bless me? Don't you know that my Doña Elvira was never wed? But it's true, you don't know.

Well, I'm telling you that since that betrothal celebration there was never again a good day in the house. Let's go, Juan. I'll tell you about it on the way."

"Tell me, tell me. What happened?"

"What happened? The day of the festivities arrived, and everything was marvelous. What a celebration, Juan! Music, sweets, fireworks, refreshments, perfumes. I'm sure that *you,* Juan, have never seen anything like it."

"Yours must be a grand household!"

"Grand! How can I tell you? I kept going back into the hall again, carrying a decanter, passing a tray, clearing away the dirty goblets. But what does all that matter now? The festivities were ruined, and to this day we don't know exactly why. Of course there've been plenty of rumors. But the only sure thing is that the bridegroom left unexpectedly. The bride had grown pale, and her efforts to hide her confusion could no longer stop people from whispering. Yes, the festivities went on. But from then on nothing went right. Something had happened. Until, a while later—I couldn't say how long, very long it seemed to me—they came to deliver a small casket from Don Felipe, the absent bridegroom, and they placed it in Doña Elvira's hands. That broke up the party. I can still see her—she held it tight to her breast and, without even opening it, fled to her room. The music stopped, and soon after, the old master (may he rest in peace!) asked one of his kinsmen to announce that his daughter was indisposed and see the guests to the door. As you can imagine, there's been a lot of gossip about the little casket—nothing is known for certain. But from that time on there was only silence, sighing, and grief in the house, weariness and sorrow. The young lady trying to seem calm. The old man pacing the galleries, up and down, day after day, his hands always clasped behind his back, looking as though he was losing his mind. Until this plague finally cut short his life and his troubles. And now, she too! Why, why her, Juan, with no other sin than her beauty?"

"None but that, truly, my son," Juan de Dios agreed tersely. Antón, with a gleam of fright amid his tears, would have liked to plumb those words, but the saint, placing a hand on his head, reassured him at once: "Don't cry, child. Listen, I couldn't go off with you now and leave all these people waiting at the door. But I'll give you others who will accompany you and will watch over your patient far better than I could."

So he went in search of Felipe and Fernando Amor, and he charged them with caring for a plague-stricken woman to whose house the boy would show them. The three of them set out without delay. In his haste and anxiety, Antoñico could hardly have been expected to recognize in the miserable and crippled appearance of one of the humble servitors now following his steps toward Doña Elvira's dwelling the proud gentleman who had disappeared in the middle of the betrothal festivities. As for Don Felipe, never, neither then nor at any other time, had he taken the slightest notice of the page of his abandoned bride. They went on together, each without recognizing or even suspecting who the other was. But Don Fernando, seeing the boy for the first time, felt in his presence some sort of inexplicable, perplexing, and painful presentiment. Silent, lost in thought, they crossed the deserted city. Their steps resounded in alleyways, before closed windows; at every corner dogs would flee; only the water and the sky and the birds of the air seemed innocent in Granada. They walked without saying a word. They advanced and, as they advanced, the oppression grew in their hearts. Their hearts were near bursting in their chests when, having reached a street familiar to them all, their guide stopped before the dreaded door, stepped into the entryway, pushed open the wrought-iron gate, and went into the courtyard. The two men exchanged looks of fright. They wavered but an instant: neither of them faltered in the trial. Up the stairs, they kept on together until they reached the bedchamber for which, once, their hostile hearts had beat with one accord.

It seems useless to proceed. What matters has been said. They found Doña Elvira already dead in the deserted house. Upon seeing her, they fell to their knees at either side of her body and commended her soul to God, while Antoñico, writhing at the foot of the bed, wailed and sobbed. Don Fernando had the sad privilege of wrapping her in her shroud with his own hands. Meanwhile, his useless arms hanging down, Don Felipe contemplated the horrible ravages of death. What anguish! Upon her withered bosom there shone a little cross of gold.

The pestilence passed, leaving Granada more desolate than repentant. It had been as a bucket of water dumped on a raging bonfire: smarting and injured, the fire complains and begins to let up. It yields, it seems about to succumb—only to recover later with even greater ferocity. All that fury, scarcely checked by the plague, was to explode years later in the rebellion of the Moriscos, whose outcome brought about the prostration in which, to this very day, the old realm languishes. However, a few, scared by the experience, disillusioned or forewarned by it, sought a new life alongside the master Juan de Dios, thus enlarging the small community that, following his example, had fought against the plague, conquered fear, and saved the name of mankind without having its pious heroism threatened by the pestilence: for not one of those selfless persons—as was reported with wonder and attributed to miracle—had been marked by its hand. And this sign of blessing was what most moved the people in favor of the holy brotherhood.

Among all his followers, Juan de Dios always secretly preferred these two gentlemen I have spoken of here, Don Felipe
and Don Fernando Amor, his helpmates in the hardest tasks.
And when he felt the hour of his passing draw near, he chose
them to be the only witnesses to his death. Calling them to
his side, he asked them to help him out of bed, for he had
reached the end of his strength. Embracing Felipe's neck,
supported by Fernando's arms, he raised his frail body; and
kneeling on the esparto mat, his elbows leaning on the straw
mattress, and a crucifix clasped between his hands, just as he
can be seen in the painting, he prayed until the end, while off
in a corner the two brothers wept in silence.

From Granada the saint's renown soon spread throughout
all Christendom, and it also reached the place where he was
born, Montemor o Novo, in Portugal. There, many testified
at the time that, on the day the blessed João de Deus came
into the world, among other miracles, a great light had been
seen in the sky, and the church bells had pealed although no
man had tolled them.

❧❧ The Invalid

"**R**uy Pérez is back at last,"
the king's parched lips whispered, and his eyelids dropped
again over his dilated pupils. Piercing the heavy rumble of the
watermill, the sound of a hunting horn, barely audible, then
drowned by the stream, had reached his ears from the woods
beyond. Now he was waiting for the splatter of the horses in
the mud; next, the sound of their hooves, muffled by the dry
leaves on the path; and, at last, the metallic clink of their
steps as they clapped across the courtyard stones.

Motionless, his head bent back, arms and legs extended,
the king waited with infinite patience. Outside, the comings
and goings in the stable, the creak of hinges and bolts, the
confused, irritated uproar of an argument; and, finally, closer
and closer on the stairs, the footsteps of his huntsman. As
soon as he appeared, Don Enrique asked:

"Tell me, Ruy Pérez, what's happened to my sorrel mare?
She's come back limping."

Without responding, the huntsman slowly closed the chamber door and held up before his master's bed a beautiful heron

Enrique III (1379–1406), sometimes called the Sickly, the Ailing, or the
Sufferer, succeeded his father, Juan I, to the throne of Castile and León at
the age of eleven. The first years of his reign, chronicled by Pedro López de
Ayala, were marked by civil war between the upper and lower aristocracy.

31

he had bagged. Then he dropped the trophy upon a bench and answered:

"It was nothing, sire. Her left forefoot was pierced by a thorn. The farrier's tending to her now. But how quickly my lord recognized it to be his mare!"

"Ah, Ruy Pérez, you devil! Riding and riding all day long. And for what?"

A weak blaze of anger raised the king on his couch. Hoisting himself up on a dry arm whose elbow thrust itself into the straw mattress, he arched his trunk and lifted up his forehead. But the effort was too much for him and his head sank back onto the pillow.

Then his nurse, Estefanía González, who had not moved all afternoon, stirred in her corner, and went to cover Don Enrique. Her quick hands arranged the folds of the blanket and the damp hair on the sick man's burning brow. He shot her a pitiful smile: "Silly old woman, Mother Estefanía!" And he was still, while she withdrew to her place without uttering a word. The king needed only the presence, the mere, mute presence of Nurse Estefanía, whose breasts had nourished his frail infancy, to feel himself supported. It was something like a renewal of the roots of life, like the ebb of those warm waves that, twenty-one years back, the woman's robust body used to send into the little body of the newborn child with the throbbing of her milk. But who, at that time, could have imagined what would come to pass in just a few short years? The nature of the evil spell was never determined at the Court; but the fact is that at the same time, within the space of days, a malignant fever scorched the bones of the infant king, ruining his health forever, and his wetnurse aged prematurely. She who had been buxom and graceful lost her vigor and her mind; her limbs wasted away, and she began to rave. They say that when he saw her in such a miserable state, her other son—her real one, the son of her flesh, that Enrique González who had grown up in the castle courtyards protected from excessive taunts by the threats of the king, ever ready to shield with his authority his foster brother's defenselessness—they say that that wretched Enriquillo González burst out laughing with rare joy when he saw his mother plunged into insanity, as though he wanted to let everybody know that she was his again, and he was joining her in those shadows, after having felt himself rejected, deprived of his natural nourishment, put aside and passed over in the interest of the royal prince. The prince, on the other hand, had cried in his bed, his head under the covers, for hours on end, in his grief at feeling himself abandoned by his nurse, who was forsaking him when he most needed her. But he had to resign himself, and he soon found consolation. Clearly, in her deranged state she was no longer the same, she was scarcely a ghost of her former self. She could not oversee the household, nor enliven it with her sayings as before; but at least she was there, she stayed close to the Invalid, mute and still, keeping him company. And only when, from time to time, she would burst into inhuman screams, did they have to remove her from his bedchamber and take her to be locked up in a tower. But this occurred only now and then, with diminishing frequency, and it had even seemed as if the malady might finally abandon her.

So the old woman sat herself down again on her stool, next to the window, while Ruy Pérez also lowered himself onto the bench, pushing aside the heron he had offered the king. He stretched out his tired legs and, after a pause, informed Don Enrique:

"My lord, today I learned something that worries me: Alonso Gómez, with all his men, has entered the service of the bishop Don Ildefonso."

"What? How did you find out? Can the news be true?" The

king knew very well that it had to be true. More than once in the past few months he had been disturbed by the extended absences of his vassal, elusive and evasive, and if he had never inquired, it was because he was afraid to know. But the desolation of his soul still sought support in the delays of doubt: "Is the news true?" he repeated with dismay. And then, without awaiting confirmation, his mouth went bitter with the remark: "God help me! Yet another defection!"

But his huntsman would not let him escape into the consolation of complaint:

"Sire, Alonso Gómez has wages owing him now for the past three years."

"Yours too, Ruy Pérez, yours too are owed you, and you have not abandoned me."

"My lord, if you abandon your people, and you are king, how can you expect your vassals not to abandon you?"

Don Enrique said nothing in reply. In the silence of the chamber, his anxious breathing could be felt. He half closed his eyes and was hoping to take shelter in sleep when the harsh voice of his huntsman pursued him again, grumbling:

"No, the falcons of the king of Castile will not want for care so long as Ruy Pérez is alive. What is wanted, indeed, is that the king not fail us in our want."

Shortly thereafter Don Enrique felt the thud of the door closing behind his huntsman, the sound of his footsteps disappearing down the stairs. And nothing more. Time passed. He began to feel drowsy again—the ringing of the blacksmith's hammer, the acrid smell of scorched hoof besieged his dozing senses—when a dog, emerging from beneath his bed, approached to sniff his hand, which was dangling outside the sheet. Twitching at the moist contact with the dog's nose, the king's hand rose slowly to caress the animal's head. But it groped in the air without finding it: the dog had already moved away to smell the heron abandoned on the bench.

"This sickness clings to me as the mastiff clings to the wild boar's ear, and I cannot tear it from my flesh. And how hard this winter in the lands of Burgos is on an ill man!" Don Enrique mused in a soft voice, making a lament of his reflections. "Everything seems dead. And I, poor me! I, the king of Castile, am I to waste away in this bed of torment? My limbs are numb. . . ." After a pause, he went on with his plaint, now directing his broken voice toward Estefanía: "Tell me, nurse: wouldn't it do me good to get up for a while, to change my position?" And then, impatiently: "Speak! Answer! I cannot believe that you don't understand me, sitting there still as a stone, a sly stone that stares and says nothing."

A slight flush of anger colored his pale cheeks for a moment, only to vanish at once. Drawing off the covers by himself, with a nervous tug, he flung himself from his bed and, faltering, proceeded to settle himself in the great armchair placed by the window. Only then did his nurse come to spread a mantle over his shoulders and to tuck its edges around his muffled body.

"You cover me, you bundle me up like a baby. That's what you know how to do. That's all that's left of you, nurse. And that, too, is all that's left of me."

The king's voice was lost in the painful wheezing issuing from his chest. In a little while, his agitation too began to subside, and at last he was quiet, his eyes gazing blankly through the window. From where he sat he could make out the deserted courtyard, enclosed by a strong wall over whose edge appeared a row of black poplars stripped of their leaves. Above, an overcast sky. And at the back, in a corner of the courtyard, a board that was rotting in the damp. Tired, Don Enrique collected his wandering gaze and let his eyes fall upon the thin hands lying in his lap. "To-day Ruy Pérez brought me a heron," his thoughts shuffled indolently. "A splendid heron. There it is. A royal heron!" I wonder what day it is. The day is ending. Night is falling now, falling."

At that moment, the familiar laugh of his foster brother, the laugh of Enrique González, exploded outside and again drew the king's attention toward the courtyard. There he was, frolicking with a groom. The man was carrying a sack on his back, and Enrique González had pulled him by the arm until he had made him lose his balance. And while the groom, back on his feet, was cursing and trying to wipe his muddy hand on the idiot's mop of hair, the latter lifted the sack in his husky arms: he had more than enough strength to heave it onto his shoulders and, thus laden, to run toward the stable, ahead of the groom who, half furious, half amused, followed his strutting figure. One after the other, they disappeared through the door at the back, and in the deserted courtyard there remained only a double row of footprints, interrupted by a muddy skid mark in a swirl of tracks. Don Enrique sat there remembering that hefty youth who was the same age as he, but who had grown so very much, and whose enormous hands were forever moving, seizing everything in sight. "Just look at him there, in the snow and in the cold," he mused, "bursting with energy. In a little while he'll go out to cast his nets in the brooks, and he'll come back proud as can be, his big hands reddened from the pinpricks of the ice, and his sack full of crayfish. He'll sit down by the hearth, he'll boil them in a pot. He won't understand the jeers of the grooms and, without answering them, he'll keep on sucking at his crayfish until, at last, he decides to lie down to sleep in a corner of the kitchen. And ten, twenty, thirty years from now he'll still be doing the same thing. His guffaws will resound in the courtyard just as they do today. Until God disposes otherwise. And I? When will I be called to the bosom of God? For what do I do? Turn over and over in that bed, and turn over and over in my imagination things that have no remedy. Over and over, until God wills otherwise. Would it not be better . . . ?"

Exasperated, he grasped the bell cord and sounded the bell loudly. Then, his hands fallen and his eyes fixed on the door, he waited. Light steps on the stairs announced the arrival of a page.

"Have Ruy Pérez come up immediately."

"My lord, Ruy Pérez has gone out again. He's not in the castle."

The king sank into so lengthy a silence that the few words he had exchanged with the boy seemed unbelievably remote, and the latter, standing at the door, thought he had been forgotten.

"My lord," he whispered.

"Well, then, have Rodrigo Alvarez come," was the order that dismissed him at last.

When, after some time, the door opened again, it was to admit a white-haired man, bearded and of grave demeanor.

"How is it, Rodrigo Alvarez," Don Enrique said to him, as soon as he appeared, "how is it that the king must spend his life alone, with no one to attend him, except for poor Estefanía, who is so in need of attention herself?"

"You know very well, my lord. Your nurse is the one person you will have at your side. Nobody else dares enter this chamber unless he is summoned. Besides, you also know that each of us is busy with his work, and that that's the best service we can all do the king, in times like these and with things the way they are."

"Sit down here beside me, Rodrigo Alvarez, my friend. You see that my health is improving. I want you to put me abreast of all that has happened recently."

The old man stroked his beard and, after a studied pause, began to speak:

"In truth, Don Enrique, I should not like to burden a sick man's repose with such harsh concerns. For were you to ask it of me, I could only give you bad tidings. But what use would it be to hear them, sire, when we've already sought every possible remedy?"

"Speak, I say."

Then his steward, in a mercilessly insistent speech, slow, meticulous, precise, began to relate the misdeeds that the lords of the realm had been committing, without respite, against the rights of the Crown. Forests destroyed, flocks stolen, towns despoiled, revenues usurped, vassals seduced away or harassed, serfs oppressed—all this gradually began to take form and pile up in the implacable wealth of details recited by the indefatigable and formal steward, as the debris of a ruined bastion piles up at the base of its crumbling structure.

Don Enrique could scarcely follow the tangle of facts that his servant reported with an overwhelming abundance of circumstances, names, and dates. One intrigue had been discovered by mere chance; another treacherous act had been denounced by a commoner, angry at being mistreated. The king trembled, as one who feels himself watched and observed from a hundred different points, without being able to see those who lie in wait.

"Enough!" he said. "Enough!" he shouted, pushing the heap of infamies back with his hands. The steward cut his account short, and remained silent. The king's hands had drawn into their hollow his heavy forehead, his aching brow.

"If God grants me strength, this summer all will be put in order."

It pleased God to grant him strength. When the rigors of the cold had passed, Don Enrique began to feel better. He had his beard combed and his nails polished, and soon he began going out into the countryside on brief hunting trips. More than in the still weak and unsteady force of his own body, he could see his recovery reflected in the people around him: as the beasts of the forest abandon their lairs in the silent snows, and even make bold to show their muzzles in the village, but flee again to their dens at the least sign of alarm, so too, when the king raised his eyes, overcoming his ailment, all the eyes that had been besieging him on the sly went back into hiding. And it was an infinite number of eyes, it was all the beings of the forest, it was all the people of the realm, it was the entire world that was spying on his movements and was anxiously watching the changes in his breathing.

Don Enrique strained his wits, looking for means with which to restore the authority of the Crown. But the vigorous action that he would finally undertake to bring this about, and which, for a moment, seemed destined to straighten the twisted course of his affairs, began to gestate unbeknownst to him. In fact it was something that had been there, buried, for years; something that had been incubated in the bosom of his fevers and his endless vigils; something ripened, known, awaited. And yet, now, as it rose up and took shape and started to move—like a snake that, until the moment its quiet slumber stirs, might have been mistaken for the dry branch of a tree—it revealed itself to be the fruit of conditions still unknown to him.

Thus, on one of those late spring days when the king had

gone out hunting, and when, toward evening, between joyous
and fatigued from the exertions of the day, he was starting
home with his retinue, back in the depths of the castle,
among the pleasantries of the coarse servants whiling away
their spare time gathered around the hearth, the first fibers of
the stuff with which the event would be woven had already
begun to be spun. The king rode on completely unawares, but
each step of his silent ride brought him closer to the only act
of strength he would perform during his reign, and for whose
consummation the unfortunate man would have to muster all
his energy.

If we want to know about this act from its very beginnings,
we shall have to descend into the kitchens and consent to
listen to the simple, rough, and vulgar conversation of the
common folk. Its starting point had been a casual question
muffled in a kitchen boy's yawn: When were they going to fix
supper? "That," replied the cook, "you must ask the honorable steward. He's the one who can tell you. Though if you
take my advice, you won't waste your strength trying to find
out, in case there's nothing for you to restore it with later."
The laughter of a few made the boy angry; but, encouraged by
them, his master went on with the jest: "Don't laugh, he's
hungry." And he asked, "Tell me, lad, are you hungry?"

"It's nobody's business whether I am or not. That's my own
business. But I see that it's almost night, and the king will
soon be here."

"Well, fine! That's great news! Listen, there won't be any
supper today. What do you say to that? What do you think of
it? Have you never heard that even a king might be so poor as
to have nothing to put in his mouth? Well, cheer up! As far as
that's concerned, we are all imitating the King of Heaven, the
poorer the more glorious. Today we shall all fast together with
the king of Castile, and that will be a penance for our sins."

"What jests are these, Master Kettle?" the grave voice of the blacksmith rebuked him from the doorway. "The king's condition is becoming far too sad for us to make jokes at his expense."

"Do you think I'm joking? I was telling this boy to prepare to fast, for he's old enough now to observe the precept. And I'm instructing him as well in the example of Our Savior, lest it enter his head to make light of the king Don Enrique on seeing him reduced to such misery. Where have you been? I've said there's no supper and there *is* none. These are facts, not jests. If it distresses you so, you and any others, and if only to stop this lad from yawning, why don't you, Maroto, since you're connected with that holy house, why don't you go up to His Grace's doors and see if the worthy bishop's servants will pass you a bowl of leftovers from the banquet that their master held yesterday? You can beg these alms in the name of your own master. Why shouldn't the king of Castile go begging?"

"A fine bishop God has given us!" exclaimed the one named Maroto. And after a studied pause, he began to recount to his companions details of the feast at which he had helped to serve the day before. A well-traveled fellow, he knew how to make people listen. With words and gestures, he praised the opulence of the banquet offered to the lords of the realm by the prelate, exaggerating the great abundance of victuals, the greed, and the wastefulness. Next, in a low voice and sententious tone, he pointed out that all that gluttonous frenzy was but a prelude to that of their hearts: for the potentates of Castile had assembled at the table of the bishop Don Ildefonso not so much to stuff their bellies as to carve up the realm, dismember it and divide its pieces among themselves, despoiling the Invalid.

"When it was about time for dessert, the bishop began to ease into the question, and all were hanging on his lips. You

know how skillful he is—he's a very learned man. And moving about in the livery of the house, I watched him without
missing a word. If you haven't heard him, you can't imagine
such a marvel . . ."

"But what did he say?" someone interrupted.

"What did he say? Ah! I never tired of watching his hand,
bobbing about in front of him like a wild pigeon, perched in
the sun, fluffing and preening its feathers. And his face—what
dignity! And those words that ran fast and thick from his
mouth, like sheep from a pen! My friends, I never took my eye
off him. And so I was able to see when still nobody else had
that something was wrong with him. Others didn't notice it,
but I did. The flock of words pressed against his lips and, once
they'd passed through the gate, spilled out helter-skelter,
while his hand, starting like a frightened bird, stayed still for a
moment and then began to flutter restlessly. Nobody noticed,
and he was able to go on speaking. But I didn't take my eye off
him, and I saw the drops of sweat flow from his reddened
forehead. More and more drops that, soaking his eyebrows,
poured from his face like a flood of tears. It looked as if he
might faint. Until . . . bang! His speech was cut off again,
and this time there was no way to hide it. He stood up, and
that ruddy face of his paled till it was blue. Everyone looked at
him in astonishment, and the words he spoke then, on his
feet, and in a very slow voice, were these: 'Well, my lords, in
order that my dignity not inhibit your judgment nor influence
your decision, I'll spare you my presence and leave you in the
company of my words.' And at once, pushing back his chair,
which he knocked over on leaving, he fled from the dining
hall, paying no attention to their pleas. The servants whose
duty it was to follow him had to run—yes, run!—after His
Grace through the gallery, all the way to his closet. When,
some time later, he returned to the hall, by then composed,

relieved, but still blue in the face, it was impossible for him to resume his speech. The lords had in the meanwhile finished off the wine, and the wine in turn had finished off the lords."

Maroto was silent, relishing the impression produced by his account, while his listeners considered his words. Only that kitchen boy whose question about supper had opened the conversation now inquired again as to why His Grace had left the dining hall so suddenly. A chorus of guffaws greeted the lad's perplexity.

"For God's sake, they're always making fun of me!" he said in annoyance.

The laughter waned, and over it the blacksmith's grave voice commented:

"Well, there's certainly no danger of accidents like that occurring in *this* house. As for the worthy prelate, it seems he doesn't learn from experience. Remember that time, almost three years ago, when in the middle of high mass he had to leave the altar, giving rise to rumors about his keeping the fast? But, in short, master," he added, now addressing the cook, "are we really going to fast, when it isn't a fast day? Decide what must be prepared and served, be it a little or a lot, for it's late and no doubt Don Enrique is about to return."

"What's to be served? And what *is* to be served? Come here, lad," shouted the cook to another boy who was in a corner braiding rope. "Come tell whoever wants to hear what you got today when the steward sent you in search of provisions."

"All I brought back was insults," the errand boy replied. "Neither meat nor bread. And they even tried to hurl the weights at my head when I asked if by chance the king's word is no longer worth an ounce of beef. It's silver they want, not words."

Silence fell. At last, someone reflected:

"We had to get to this point sometime or other. With the

king sick, not strong enough to move about by himself, much
less command the respect of bad vassals who refuse to pay
what they owe and steal what isn't theirs to boot, what else
could we expect but this disgrace? My poor master, who in his
own realm is a captive heavy with chains! Here he comes
now. How it pains me that he must come back to this."

Indeed, outside was heard the stamping of the hunters who
were arriving and dismounting in the courtyard. Then they
went up to the great hall, and Don Enrique ordered supper
brought in. That was the moment when his hands touched
upon the first fibers of the web and began to get tangled in it.
Time passed, then more time, and the king's order was not
carried out. Disgruntled, impatient, irritated, he had to repeat
it three times, and when he was on the very brink of rage, the
cook, his countenance unsettled, appeared in his presence to
inform him: "My lord, we have no supper."

"And how's that? What's happened?" shouted Don Enrique. "Where's my steward? Send him here immediately!"
Don Enrique was tired and hungry; at times the tone of his
anger took on sorrowful inflections, shades of desolation. And
the men of his retinue, who were moving about, unbuckling
their spurs, arranging their pouches and saddlebags, and talking over the day, turned around when they heard him, paid
attention, and waited expectantly.

Now the cook tried to explain: the steward, Rodrigo Alvarez, had gone out with a small detachment to collect as best he
could something of what was owed the king, and he had sworn
upon leaving not to return without bringing back some
money. He paused, took heart at Don Enrique's astonishment, and added: "Sire, our money ran out some time ago.
Today we ran out of credit as well."

All eyes were upon the young king: a hot wave rose through
his pale cheeks to his eyes, which stared absently through the

window at the darkened countryside. After a long, painful moment, they saw him remove his cape and hand it to the cook. "Send this out to be pawned, Juan."

The man bowed as he took the garment and left the lords waiting silently. "Here, go quickly, run and pawn this," he ordered a messenger as soon as he had gone down to the kitchen. "The king has given up his own outer warmth so that we can warm our insides. Go and trade wool for mutton. And God grant that it not be too tough, so we'll have some peace and quiet."

The boy ran to the city, went around the crooked streets behind the cathedral, and placed the cape in the hands of a Jew who, unfolding the cloth, examined it inside and out and asked, "Where did you steal this?" At last, turning his back, he took a piece of gold from a drawer and handed it to the boy without another word.

Supper was a somber affair. At first, everyone was silent, devouring the dish that the cook had prepared in great haste. But when the gravy, seasoned with rosemary and thyme, and the tart local wine had fortified their hearts without dissipating their gloom, they began to speak angrily, bitterly, of the contrast between the king's present poverty and the insolent magnificence of his great vassals. The discussion had begun in low tones, among neighbors; but soon it spread out across the tabletop like a pitcher spilling over, and whispers at first subdued by wrath reached a vibrant pitch of indignation. Its light lent, above all, a crude brilliance to the details of the feast that had been celebrated the day before in the palace of the bishop Don Ildefonso. With injured vehemence they brought up examples of unbelievable dissipation, scandalous merriment and pagan extravagance.

The king ate silently, lost in thought. But when supper was over, he retired with Ruy Pérez, his huntsman, and they decided to devise a stratagem that would curtail the power of the emboldened nobles. So as to arrange the particulars of the plan without hindrance, another hunting party was organized to consist only of men selected by Ruy Pérez himself.

And thus, two days later, those summoned to take part in the plot set off before the break of day and rode about a league and a half. While the servants went on ahead with the dogs, the lords stayed behind, clustered tightly around the king, to discuss how it would be done, and when. Once this was agreed upon, settled, and arranged in detail, they dismounted in a wood and gathered in the shade of an oak tree to rest before the beaters began to drive the game. Now that everything was set, they speculated with nervous jubilation about the consequences of the coup, which would restore to the king a power "gnawed away by the rats of treason," punishing the arrogance and abuses of the magnates.

Detached from the circle, Don Enrique listened to the noisy chatter of his friends, who were interrupting one another and passing the wine as they celebrated in advance the success of their plan. And when, after a while, the king tried to make his way into the enthusiastic group, he had to rest his hand insistently on the shoulder of Ruy Pérez who, at that moment, was holding the wineskin high to catch a fine stream of the transparent redness in his gullet. Then they all hastened to offer the king something to eat. But Don Enrique made a sign to his huntsman, who gave the order: the horns were sounded, the men assembled, and Ruy Pérez commanded a sudden return. The news spread at once among the servants: the king had been taken ill.

Then, step by step as had been planned, the show of strength was carried out that was to exhaust the strength of the Invalid. Two weeks had elapsed since that day, with the castle gates shut tight, and now all the lords of the realm were arriving, each from his lands and villages. As the grandees' retinues gathered in the rear courtyards, the rumor of the king's death grew thicker among the men. Equerries and footmen looked after their beasts while harassing the stableboys with shouts and insults, but the magnates' servants and squires talked with each other about the reasons for the assembly that had been convened and its possible consequences. Nobody knew anything with certainty, but they all concealed their ignorance beneath a show of reserve. And so the atmosphere of mourning grew increasingly dense; it lent concern to their faces and moderation to their voices.

In the meantime, the grandees, assembled in the ceremonial hall, were whispering together near the windows in groups that would dissolve and merge with one another each time the door of the room was opened to admit a new potentate. The last to arrive was the grand master* of Santiago, Don Martín Fernández de Acuña. Over his armor he wore the habit of his Order. He stopped in the doorway and greeted the assemblage with loud joviality. Seeing among them his cousin and brother-in-law, the admiral Don Juan Sánchez de Acuña, he opened his arms and embraced him, asking for news from home. "We haven't seen each other for three years, brother," he said. And then, taking him off into a corner and lowering his voice, he asked him what he knew about why they had been summoned there. "It seems," the admiral explained, "that the king is about to give up the ghost, and he wishes to make a public testament. But nothing is known for certain." They remained silent a moment: the grand master, with his head held high above the white fringe of his carefully trimmed beard; the admi-

*The head of a military Order of knighthood.

ral, his eyes lowered, absentmindedly contemplating the nails of his left hand. Near them another small group was recalling the ups and downs of the king's health, trying to fathom the designs of Providence. "After being attacked by the malady," someone there reported, "his countenance grew ugly and his spirit turned sour, as though wishing to keep pace with his weak body, incapable of any useful undertaking and even unfit for any joy."

"I've heard it said by those who've seen him recently that death is painted on his face already, and that the very foulness of his breath proclaims how he carries it with him in his body," another intervened. "I understand that we've been called to hear his last will."

At that moment, the door flew open. All conversations were cut short; all faces turned toward it; all eyes converged on that spot. And they saw that very same king Don Enrique, whose agony they had expected to witness, enter with a slow and steady step, fully armed, his bloodshot eyes blazing in a face white with rage. He came forward, cutting through their stupor to the center of the hall. Standing there, after an icy pause, in a composed tone and a slow voice that concealed his agitation, the king addressed his vassals:

"My lords," said he, "before telling you why I have assembled you, I wish to ascertain of each man one thing, and it is this: How many kings have each of you known in Castile?"

The magnates, baffled, looked at one another in astonishment and, unable to imagine what the melancholy king was driving at with his strange question, were silent. But the king persisted, in an even softer and slower voice:

"Come, my lords: how many kings has each of you known in Castile?"

It was only after a long pause that the constable Don Al-

49 The Invalid

fonso Gómez Benavides, leaning on the arm of his grandson, who had accompanied him to the gathering, spoke and said:

"My liege, it would seem unnecessary to inquire of each one what I, as the eldest, can answer in the name of all. Five kings have my many years known in Castile. When the long course of my life began, Don Alfonso had the realm, and he enlarged it without respite or repose. Envious of his glory, a plague cut short his life, preventing him from extending his estates to the magnitude of his greatness. And Envy, now mistress of the realm, disturbed and weakened it in the struggles between two brother kings, Don Pedro and Don Enrique, your grandfather, whose name and crown, my lord, are yours. I next beheld the reign of your father, Don Juan;* and finally, sire (and perhaps your mind, too young at the time, has not retained the memory of the day when I first kissed your infant hands and called you King), finally . . . I wish indeed that my tired eyes might close forever without seeing another. Five kings are enough for a single lifetime.

Curbing his anger out of respect, Don Enrique had listened to the old man's speech, while in the interval the other nobles had time to ponder their predicament. But those last words, touching to the quick the false pretext for that assemblage, inflamed the royal ire again with their imprudence. And so, no sooner had the constable closed his lips than the king retorted:

"Five reigns are enough indeed for a single lifetime, and it is hard to bear the varying rule of each. How would it be if,

*Alfonso XI was king of Castile and León from 1312 to 1350. His son, Pedro I, reigned from 1350 until 1369, when he was killed at Montiel by his half-brother Enrique de Trastamara, who ruled as Enrique II from 1369 to 1379. Enrique's son, Juan I, was king from 1379 to 1390. (For more information about the first three, see "The Embrace.")

instead of having reigned one after the other, those princes had all reigned together, and if instead of five they had been twenty?"

Pale with rage, the king had spoken the first words, slow and hissing, from deep in his chest. But after the pause of the first sentence his voice began to vibrate, quivering at the start of the question and growing increasingly louder until it reached the pitch of imprecation: "Well, twenty! twenty—not five—are the kings now reigning in Castile! Twenty, and even more! You, my lords, are the kings of this realm. You are the ones who hold the power and the wealth, the ones who show authority, who give the orders, who command and are obeyed. But I swear by those very ancestors of mine you named, Constable Alfonso Gómez, I swear that your false power has fallen as of this day, and will never rise up again in these lands."

The king turned his back on them. All eyes then rose from the flagstones of the floor to the crest of his helmet. When he had disappeared through the doorway, they tried to confer with one another, but they were prevented from doing so by the guards who, invading the hall, proceeded to disarm them and take them prisoner.

While his orders to despoil the insolent lords were being carried out, two servants relieved the king of his arms, undressed him, and helped him into bed. Don Enrique was trembling like a leaf, and his teeth chattered.

Summer had almost passed and autumn was on its way when the Invalid first tried to raise his head again and overcome his prostration and learn what had become of the prisoners while he had been sunk in fever and delirium. Nobody would tell him anything. But, after pressing for an answer, he came to know that they were all free and living quietly in their own dwellings. And he learned still more: he learned with stupefaction that it had been he himself, the king Don Enrique, who had decreed their freedom.

He then fell into an abyss of silence. However much he tried, he could remember nothing. And who could have come to the aid of his memory? Who? That poor Estefanía perhaps, who, sitting by his bed, was chasing away the troublesome flies?

🏛️ The Bell of Huesca

Ⅰn the days when men gave service dignity and their lives to service, because they lived for death, a monk of royal blood was plucked from the life of devotion in which he was absorbed, and exalted among men to occupy the throne.

Until that very moment, Ramiro the Monk* had been ignorant of his destiny. Born to be so, he grew up and matured in that ignorance—an ignorance different from that of the common run of mortals; for who, in truth, knows his own destiny? With presentiments, suspicions, yearnings, and anticipation, blind hands grope toward the presumed image of the future, only to weaken, and draw back, and give up, and yield to the rough forms that the rocks and crags of the world impose upon the impetuous vegetal softness of each soul. But Ramiro's soul had sprouted with its back to its destiny, looking toward another, toward an apocryphal destiny, and lifting its branches to a heaven that seemed pledged to his tonsured head as its sole glory and crown.

For the crown of his father, Sancho Ramírez, king of Ara-

---

*Ramiro II the Monk (1085?–1154), second son of Sancho V Ramírez of Aragon, who ruled from 1063 to 1094 and was succeeded by his elder son, Alfonso I the Battler. When Alfonso was killed in 1134 without an heir, Ramiro was brought from his monastery to become king.

gon, was already assigned to round the temples of the elder brother, who would then pass it on to his own descendants through lines fading away into a future peopled with noble generations, where, nonetheless, there was no place whatever for his seed as royal prince: and, so that it might not decay in obscurity, it was to be sacrificed to God in an offering of sterility. That had been established and decreed by the time Ramiro was born; Alfonso was there already, with regal obstinacy written on his still naked brow, his chest held high, his lips pressed tight, his large, stubby-fingered hands clenched, and the stride of his legs, hardened by riding, heavy and slow. He was there already, full of himself and patiently awaiting the inevitable. Power flowed, through secret streams of blood, from father to son; it came from the dead and went toward the still unborn. And Ramiro had opened his eyes to the world only to see from the shore that firm and mysterious conspiracy of the king with his first born, a conspiracy that ineluctably excluded him and drew him off into a destiny of obedience. The son of kings, his veins were swollen with the same violent and proud blood of the powerful; yet he was obliged to tame it, always to tame it, to silence it, to close its mouth, to dam it up, to subdue it always, because, though so close to power, he was a subject, and he had to temper himself to submission.

But he had found all this fixed and established at his birth, and he did not hesitate a moment: he set out in silence toward that destiny he thought was his, which nobody doubted was his, and he embraced it with his heart. He embraced it and in it he sought salvation. Disdainfully, he abandoned second place and preferred to have no place at all, to be nobody. He felt that second place had been created to vilify the vile by making them wallow in their vileness, and to break noble souls that, having resisted the corrosion of the worst acids, desperate with ambition, are driven to damn themselves with daggers or with poison. It is a place of violent temptations, of the kind that one can only escape by a flight that renounces all.

Ramiro fled and went to throw himself at the feet of God. Shrinking and bent over, hidden beneath his robe as if in the depths of a cavern, he had succeeded, after hours and months and years of struggle, in throttling his own blood and reducing it to silence. He came to abhor power, since it was not God's will that he abhor the powerful, burdened as they were with the weight of their worthy service. And pitying their honors, he prayed to Him for them—for his father, for his brother—in a supplication in which infinite compassion for the great was mixed with an equally infinite gratitude for the insignificance he had finally attained by means of the dark habit granted him by the Lord God so that he might avoid the shame of that dignity without service which had come to him at his birth.

And he had so succeeded in cleansing himself of pride that, having been requested more than once, in memory and by virtue of his royal blood, to assume an abbacy or a bishopric, Ramiro, smiling from the depths of his humility, agreed to take on that minor authority and power, only to abdicate it shortly thereafter, once his renunciation could no longer bear any tint of haughtiness. Finally, even his name and his lineage seemed completely forgotten beneath his drab habit.

It was then that the grandees of the realm came to reclaim him as king. Alfonso, the firstborn, had died, leaving no direct successor. He had, indeed, left a testament; but it was an incredible testament, which added perturbation and perplexity of mind to the upheaval caused in the realm by his death. Once the manuscript was read, curiosity had given way to surprise; surprise grew into astonishment; and astonishment degenerated into scandal. The Battler had fallen. And now, when he was no longer capable even of lifting his fearsome arm, scandal sprouted around his corpse as mushroom buttons, irrepressibly and in silence, sprout in the forest as soon as the storm is past. For who could have imagined that someone might wish to use the Orders of God so as to offend Him? Weary of battling, Alfonso bequeathed the realm to the holy swords of the Knights Templars, the Knights of the Holy Sepulcher, and the Knights of Saint John of Jerusalem: that was his will. Had he wished in so doing to extend the limits of his funeral chapel up to the frontier of his estates and convert the whole realm into a crypt for his corpse and a monument to his glory under the sacred custody of the military Orders?

At first nobody knew what to think or what to say, so difficult was it to decipher the impiety hidden beneath that cloak of piousness! Some subtle stratagem was sensed by all; no one could specify, however, precisely what the disquieting element might be, nor what made it so insufferable. But the scandal grew and grew in their consciences with the lascivious thrust of mushrooms; and the limbs of the deceased king were not yet cold within his armor when the grandees of the realm dared to raise their voices in the presence of the corpse and discuss before the catafalque itself a way to oppose his written will.

Names and lineages were examined, without reaching agreement. The ancient royal blood of some lines, diluted by mixtures and bastardies, obscured by the lusterless tenure of small seigniories or by long periods of minority in which the family had vegetated as though shaded, in circles of women and orphans, could have led them, nonetheless, to the throne. But that throne had in the meanwhile grown too grand and glorious; and if all of them, each with his estates and fiefs, were willing to serve as country lords—and that was already an honor—not one of them seemed good enough to the rest to bear on his shoulders the burden of the most exalted service and to serve as king.

In the ardor of their discussions, they eventually forgot about the testament altogether, and even about King Alfonso himself, stretched out there, huge and imposing in his armor. His broadsword lay rigid at his side; the short, hairy fingers of his hands, poking out from between the mesh of his gauntlets like a mass of enormous worms, were fast entwined; his eyes, once the terrible part of his face, were sunken, erased by the prominence of his dull, hoary blond beard, whose disorder half hid the famous scar by which people had come to recognize him and which perpetuated in the flesh of his left cheek the swift stroke that had split it from his ear to the very corner of his mouth, now black, from which a page was shooing off the stubborn flies. At his side, their whispers had gradually grown into murmurs, and their murmurs into an intemperate, bitter outcry. And their irritated voices had gone beyond irreverence to sacrilege by the body whose soul was even then accounting for having attempted to entomb the entire realm along with itself, when the bishop of Sahagún called to mind and proposed the name of the royal monk who had been his predecessor in the ministry of the diocese only to return at once to the silence of Tomeras Monastery and assume again, in keeping with his humble calling, the incomparable dignity of the soul that serves God alone.

That name rang like a revelation in the troubled ears of the grandees. The bishop's words relieved the hearts of all, and it seemed incredible that nobody had remembered it before. It was as though the passing over of Ramiro by Alfonso in his testament had had until that moment the power to suppress his very name, and even after the device of bequeathing the realm to the military Orders had been stripped away, the tacit design concealed in the empty nutshell that was his express will had insidiously persisted. Only when the right of Ramiro the Monk was invoked did they realize that the testament of Alfonso the Battler was finally null and void.

The parliament of the realm was convened in Borja. The delegates to the Commons, who had come to the city with no other news of the royal testament than that which had been deformed in passing from mouth to ear, who had talked about rumors of a plot against the great deceased king in groups in the marketplace and in the atrium of the church, and who had looked helplessly at one another when they learned the tenor of his dispositions, were filled with gladness when they heard Ramiro's name, and they accepted it.

The exaltation of the Monk lent form and substance to the thick rancor boiling in their breasts against the proud man who had presumed to close all doors behind him and perpetuate the orphan state of the people and be their last king by offering the Crown to God—so that nobody could take it without sacrilege—and surrendering it, like an offering hung on a hermitage wall, into the custody of the Orders. The exaltation of the Monk humiliated the proud king and gave joy to his subjects, who felt themselves exalted in him. But they also rejoiced because, after the violent man who had forced them to forget themselves and give all they had and give themselves, too, body and soul, to the aggrandizement of the realm, burdening them with the sacrifice that went with the glory with which he was invested, they desired the reign of a meek man, who would neither crush them with his stature nor further obligate them with an increase of territories.

To reclaim him as their prince, they went to the monastery where he was fulfilling his false destiny. And no sooner did he hear himself called, scarcely had they told him that the brother who had already been there when he was born existed no more and that the realm was asking him to take his place and to come rule over men, than a surge of terror, anguish, and happiness clouded his sight. Sweat ran from his brow, and it dampened his chest and his groin. Suddenly he thought he saw his true destiny, which, concealed from him all the years of his life, was revealed to him now in one delayed stroke; now, when his soul had already yielded to another destiny, one of obedience and renunciation. And so, while his face betrayed his terror and his weakened arms and legs gave way, his fevered blood rose in his head, his heart, his member, flooding him in waves with horror at himself.

Soon he regained his spirits and could master the pack of hounds rioting in his ears. His face said no, behind the shield of his hands opposing their pale palms to the world. Time and time again the grandees of the realm insisted, and just as many times the tonsured head again demurred, turning slowly from right to left and from left to right. No; not he; that was not his vocation. His refusal had lost the urgency of the first shock; it was serene, and filled with a bitterness that was at times transformed—perhaps corrupted—into a sort of evil enjoyment. No; not he. He had vowed to serve God in humility, with works within the reach of anyone, with the minor works of a submissive soul. Did they perhaps wish to damn him? How could he abandon the vestments of God to wield the sword of those who serve Him with the strength of their arms—he, who was used to turning violence against himself? His questions resounded in the silence, while his eyes, at once pained and ironic, looked questioningly into the eyes of counts and prelates.

But when the mouths of the latter at last pronounced and sounded in the air the words that had been in his heart from the beginning—that secret are the ways of God, and it was a divine mandate that it would be hopeless to oppose—the

Monk yielded, with a dead soul, to what in his heart he had accepted from the first moment.

Ramiro donned the purple, girded on the sword, put on spurs, and, kissing his father's crown, occupied the throne. The grandees came to kiss his hand, cold as the metal of that crown, and he who was humble had to suffer their obeisance and keep outstretched the hand that wanted to hide like a furtive animal.

He also had to take a wife. For now he knew that the future lay open to his seed like an immense womb, awaiting it with trembling eagerness so as to carry on his lineage, while the lineage of the firstborn, cut off, undone, had wasted away in three damask-covered beds where, a few months before his death, Alfonso had seen his children's flesh devoured by pox, and his illustrious name thus reduced to making its nest in a lopped branch of the family tree.

The Church released the Monk from his vows, yielding before the signs of Providence, and the Holy Father granted him permission to wed the granddaughter of the duke of Guienne, Inés de Poitiers, who would bring to Aragon her barely pubescent virginity.

Inés arrived upon a small white mare with trappings of green and gold. The bride was accompanied by her tutor, guarded by a troop of knights from her house, and followed by more than twenty mules laden with garments and gifts. So that she might reach the Court refreshed, her retinue had camped in a certain village nearly a league from Huesca, from where a brother of the new queen rode on ahead with a squire to announce her. Don Ramiro went out with his servants to wait for her at the city gates. At the sight of his bride, the king lowered his eyes; but he raised them at once, now unfeeling and hard, and looked at her from behind an impassive mask that he had fashioned for himself in haste out of the muscles of his face, and which seemed to her both troubling and horrifying. Made of faded tones of yellow, of reddish hairs clustered in thick eyebrows and in a sparse and still new beard, it was altogether too large for the trunk that bore it—short, lean-limbed, and all but buried in the bridegroom's rich attire. The cheerful innocence and deep strength of Inés' honest heart surmounted that vision at once. Overcoming her own fatigue and the weary look of her lank hair, of her lashless eyes reddened by the dust, and of her young and slightly flattened bosom, she felt and looked beautiful when the love she had stored up for her husband, and which she had learned from the birds of the forest, suddenly sprouted within her.

The royal monk had accepted his bride as part of his recently discovered destiny, but he did not want her love. Love played no part in the demands of that destiny. And so, when the moment came and Inés, dazzled by the lights, music, incense, and summer heat, awaited him, trembling, her soul astir with movements of dark and happy confusion, he went to her with the unbridled authority of a male and a king. Then, once the nuptial nights had passed, he abandoned her chamber, struggling against his own blood which all but burst his temples, which pounded in his breast and swelled his member. But must he also let himself be carried away by his blood?

The adolescent queen, now with child, had to spend night after night alone in her bed. Each time she heard Ramiro's footsteps approach her chamber door, she held her breath; but his steps passed by without stopping, time and again, as he tirelessly paced the gallery till daybreak—to the brink of madness, of a sob and a scream.

In this way the king shut himself off from a love he did not want to acknowledge and from which, on occasion, he would escape by setting out into the countryside and riding by night, first at a gallop and then slowly, walking his horse, his eyes fixed on the black mass of oak trees and his ear on the endless dialogue of the brook and the nightingale, a penetrating dialogue, but lost in shadows: like his destiny.

Each time the designs of God seemed to him more obscure; each day new thorny and flowery branches sprouted in his heart, distracting him for hours on end. He would implore the Lord that he might understand the enigma of that illusion in which He had kept him, and why He had made him abhor power only to make him powerful, and had pushed him with the irresistible gentleness of His hand toward the road of humility and obedience only to order his submissive soul to adopt the imperious attitude of the proud. For, in truth, he feared his own power far more than his subjects did, and the sense of authority that surrounded the purple lent its color to his cheeks.

His broodings scarcely left room for things from the outside: they were either too crude or too trivial, and they never met the measure of his soul. These things were not for him. He knew how to tie his sandals and to move within the confines of a cell; he also knew how to find God's countenance in the movement of the heavens, in the trembling of water, in the desolate swaying of the branch abandoned by a bird. But if he were obliged to sit down and settle a quarrel between two barons who matched greed against pride, or obstinacy against pettiness, he could scarcely keep his seat. He would decide in a moment, leaving the litigants exasperated and the Court itself vexed, and even more vexed because the justice of his decision could not be faulted: the king had made up his mind from the start, judging the dispute in the eyes of the adversaries, and judging it well; but he had not allowed them to go on at length, to practice deceit and reveal their stupidity, to dump their rancor at his feet, and each of them was forced to leave with his bundle of bad feelings like a peddler dismissed by a farmer without having had a chance to untie his wares. And always the same old story: an emissary, covered with dust and soaked in sweat, would approach his ear and breathlessly deposit there news that the king of Castile* had once again entered Aragonese lands, and that he had already taken Tarazona, or Calatayud, or Saragossa. The royal monk would look at him slowly; and when the bad tidings had finally penetrated him like a stone falling in the thick waters of a pond, he would put the matter off with a sign, only to surrender himself, perhaps, his head on his hand, to the anxious evoking of a certain gesture that had suddenly come to mind from out of the distant mists of his past, and which could have expressed his brother Alfonso's contempt when—as a boy—he stumbled upon Ramiro's infant self huddled in a corner among the servants, listening to their tales and jokes, or the heartsick anger of his father, Sancho Ramírez—years later—watching from the archway of a window his sorry skill in saddling horses.

And Inés, seeing him thus, sleepless to the point of stupor, with his cheek in the palm of his hand for hours on end, would remain silent, somewhat apart from him, not daring to interrupt his thoughts. She loved him, and all the while she understood nothing, she asked nothing, she asked herself nothing. She was always waiting for him; she would have waited years for him; she could have gone on waiting all her life. But meanwhile, time was racing by: autumn passed, then winter, and inside the queen's childlike body there had been

*Alfonso VII the Emperor (1104–57), king of León and Castile from 1126 to 1157, assumed the title of Emperor in 1135. His expansionist ambitions led him to claim primacy over Aragon. At the end of 1134 he seized Saragossa, from which he was forced to retire after gaining important concessions from Ramiro.

growing another body that dominated it voraciously, giving it the swollen look of a great earth-white spider.

The hour of delivery came, and he wished to be present. Standing by the bed, throughout the hours of an entire day he attended the ritual convulsion of the sacrificial woman, whose enormous, immobile belly caused her legs, arms, and head to shake with unfailing regularity. Finally he saw her innards part like a cleft in the earth and there emerge, laboriously, the great, dank-rooted onion on which would devolve the Crown of Aragon.

When Ramiro chose to join Petronila, his newborn daughter, in matrimony to the heir of the Castilian king, his fortunate adversary, the Aragonese lords again felt that the realm was about to be lost. Alfonso had sought to entomb it in his mausoleum out of pure arrogance and now this meek Ramiro wanted to abandon his rule, to relinquish it during his life-time, and to put them under the power of another king whose violence they had felt on their own flesh. So the grandees opposed that negative will, that subtle abdication by which the royal monk believed he could recover what he had lost by delivering what was left to the conqueror so that, in his hands, the dismembered land might be made whole. Having suffered the Battler's fist, the lords feared that of Alfonso VII of Castile. They did not agree to the betrothal; the realm denied its consent.

And only then did Ramiro realize that, while he had been living in spiritual turmoil, the men who had made him king, thinking that his meekness would leave them free to conduct their own affairs, had put their hands to the affairs of the realm; that he had lost the power he feared, the authority of which he had been ashamed; and that everything was pro-ceeding in the end as though the realm had in fact fallen to the military Orders. And he realized, too, that he had failed the mandate of God.

It is said that he spent a whole night asking Him for counsel, and for the strength to follow it. In any case, he executed his cruelty in the belief that he was obeying God. With horrible loathing, but with horrible assurance, he prepared the famous exemplary punishment; he did it, his soul filled with icy repugnance, but without a moment's hesitation. Until then, the will of God had always come to him through meditation, amid unbearable perplexities: he had had to wait patiently hour after hour, in a vigil, in the silence of the night, to glimpse it for an instant in the turnings of his thoughts, to barely sense it, imprecise as the signal made by a twig tapping on a windowpane. And never, after the exhausting wait spent watching for some subtle signs, had he been sure that he understood them aright. But this time the Lord had made His will known to him in a clear and sudden way. The mandate came to him by way of his heart, in one surge of his blood. It was his violent blood that commanded him to do the deed: blood will have blood, it longs to bathe the world in blood! And so much evidence, so clear a call, so firm a resolution lent terrible swiftness to his preparations for the sinister deed.

His instructions were scarcely credited by the servants of his household. They were too accustomed to the detachment of that pious and distracted king, who would give orders in a timid voice and immediately forget them, and of whom it was said that once, when he had asked for a glass of water, his servants, wondering whether, if they pretended to forget, he would ask again, had been astonished, an hour later, to see the king in person coming for his water to the very place where his pages were laughing over their insolent joke. And so, on learning that the Monk had summoned the executioner and his assistants and had ordered the block to be erected, when no crime had been committed nor was any sentence to be carried out, they thought instead that he had gone mad.

These preparations were made in absolute secrecy. The block was not set up in the public marketplace, but in a large hall of the palace, near the church atrium; and no one could guess the purpose, for only a few of Ramiro's intimates, and the knights of the queen's retinue who had accompanied her to Aragon and stayed at Court, took part in the swift comings and goings and the whisperings of the plot. At the appointed time, messengers bearing deceptive orders were dispatched in different directions to summon the grandees of the realm; and all was carried out with icy precision.

The first head to fall, severed by the ax, was the very old and venerable head of the prelate of Huesca. It was later said that, even as it rested on the thick stump beneath the hands of the headsman's assistant, whose fingers were rudely pushing back the dignitary's white beard, the haughty lord was still unable to believe his changed fortune, nor could he bring himself to set aside his anger for the submissive modesty with which it is decorous to appear in the presence of God.

Upon the bishop's blood, which flowed to the ground in thin, black trickles, there poured that of the rest of the grandees, one after the other. It all happened so swiftly that they scarcely had time to abandon their haughty self-assurance and assume, after their initial surprise, the attitude that each man's soul might dictate to him in the face of death. And only the lord of Barbastro paused at the threshold and turned pale and his mouth twitched and his eyes rolled wildly when he saw a little dog lick the blood still streaming from a headless trunk, in which he recognized the corpulence and garments of his own brother.

When at last there was no one left to execute, the bodies were taken away in a cart and the heads were placed on view in the atrium of the church, in the form of a bell that proclaimed the exemplary punishment dealt out by the king to those who had dared the most—as a crier explained, summoning the people with the roll of his drum. A horrified silence prevailed in the square, and lasted all day, and at night it grew deeper still. But in time not even the children looked at the fleshless heads. The only written testimony of all this can be found in the *Anales Toledanos,* * which read: "They killed the potentates of Huesca: the year was 1136."

Several months later, Aragon celebrated the solemn betrothal of Doña Petronila to Ramón Berenguer IV.[†] The bride was two years of age; the bridegroom, twenty-four.

Ramiro the Monk gave the Catalan prince, along with his daughter, the exercise of power, reserving for himself, during the seventeen more years that his mortal existence was prolonged, the title and the semblance of King. In this way, and after such disturbing and painful crises, after so much anguish and searching, after so much tormenting his soul, Ramiro finally fulfilled his original destiny, living his life at Court in that dignity without service that was appropriate, given his royal state, to the order of his birth.

* A medieval compilation of historical facts and events, in chronological order, up to the year 1391.
[†] Last count of Barcelona (1114 or 1115–62). After his betrothal to Petronila in 1137, he adopted the title Prince of Aragon.

🪶 The Impostors

So it was. Neither the warnings of his own Council of State, nor the admonitions of the king Don Felipe, exhorting him in his dual authority as statesman and as kinsman, nor even the very prudent voice of the Holy Father had sufficed to curb the impetus of that obstinate youth. And all Christendom was to see with consternation how his vertiginous destiny was fulfilled: for the star of the king Don Sebastián* fell, mowed down in the furor of thousands of scimitars, to sink into a thick pool of blood. And now, their anguish spent with time, there remained in the memory of the Christian princes—witnesses of the tender, brilliant meteor that had crossed the seas from Lisbon to Morocco in the summer of 1578—only a pious recollection of the adolescent who, against all advice, had gone there to be swallowed up with his army of rioters and rakes.

But that was now, after time had gone by and their horror

---

*Sebastião I (1554–78) of Portugal succeeded his grandfather João II to the throne at the age of three. Until he was declared of age in 1568, the government was directed first by his grandmother, then by his great-uncle Cardinal Dom Henrique. A headstrong young man with no interest in women, Sebastião was obsessed with the idea of a great holy crusade against the infidel. Defying all advice, including that of the Pope, he drained his country's resources to fit out a huge expedition that sailed in June 1578 from Lisbon to Morocco, where the Portuguese force was destroyed in a four-day had been vanquished. For when it happened, when news of the disaster reached Portugal, an extraordinary silence had spread across all the land: the entire realm fell silent, filled with inexpressible sympathy for the prince who, possessed with holy zeal, had succumbed to the power of the infidels because he could not master his noble impatience—the same impatience that, a few years earlier, had, to the displeasure of some and the astonishment of all, driven him to test the strength of the defenses guarding the capital of the monarchy by attacking it with his own fleet; the same impatience that the wisest men were wont to censure as madness, shaking their heads sadly, but in which the finest youths of Portugal and with them all the common people thought they saw the sign and promise of a mettle exceeding, for the moment, the skill of his still childish hands. And in the general stupefaction and confusion occasioned by his loss, only his uncle, the regent Cardinal Don Enrique, had withdrawn—paling at the news—to the palace oratory to pray with heartfelt sorrow for the salvation of his soul; for he alone had detected the despair hidden beneath the gallant daring of the youthful king; he alone had understood the Alcazarquivir expedition to be what in truth it was: a magnificent suicide. Through the tears that blurred them, his faded eyes seemed to see, again and again, the stubborn prince shutting his own eyes, hard and strange, clenching his teeth, and spurring on his white mare to deliver

---

battle near the inland town of Alcazarquivir. Cardinal Dom Henrique was regent until his death in 1580, leaving the throne vacant. Sebastião's uncle, the powerful Felipe II, king of Spain from 1556 to 1598, claimed it and was recognized by the Portuguese parliament in 1581, thus beginning a period of sixty years of Hapsburg rule of Portugal.

In the first twenty years after the Alcazarquivir disaster, the messianic hopes on the part of many Portuguese that their young king had not died and would return to reclaim the throne gave rise to a strong wave of Sebastianism, a sentiment that would linger on in Portugal for several centuries.

unto death his accursed flesh, which refused to beget in the flesh of woman a successor to the throne.

But years had passed; and their course had relegated to history the adventure that had once made an awestruck Europe hold its breath, and which, by cutting off the dynasty in its bloom, was to convey the realm from the hands of an old prelate to those of the great Felipe. The Portuguese were now living under the Crown of Spain, and, all their thirst for power dammed up under its calm zenith, the image of the African rout began to vanish for them like a mirage. No doubt the ardent, inexperienced, and frenzied figure of the king who had disappeared with his host in the foolhardy enterprise continued to fill their hearts with nostalgia. His name and his likeness were linked in every home to the name and likeness of a son lost in his company. Brothers who, from the balconies of their envious childhood, had perhaps waved good-bye to the ships of the expeditionary fleet, were already grown men; by their own age they could reckon the age of those who had gone off in their youth, and thus they occupied their idle imaginations, maturing and aging in their minds the scarcely remembered features of the missing. For was it not still a time in which each family could allow itself the hope of seeing its own son return—in the midst of so much death—safe and sound from captivity? Yes, the next hand to knock at the door could still be the hand of that son. As it could also be the hand of the king Don Sebastián in person. But time, as it wore on, slowly changed this hope into a melancholy custom.

It was then that the impostors began to appear.

True as it is, and as well documented, the story of the pastry-cook from Madrigal nonetheless belongs to the sort of adventures that can only be told and hearkened to after people have turned a deaf ear to good sense. It demands that we bring to bear upon it our highest powers of recollection, refined until converted into pure imagination, and, after that, transform imagination back into a memory of the stupendous case. It is, as I said, a documented case: official records bear witness to it. And yet, any attempt to investigate, draw inferences, or make conjectures about the steps that led the protagonist from obscurity to the public stage proves futile; it is useless to ask how he managed to approach the gates of the realm, to reach the very stairway to the throne and set foot upon its steps—only to have them turn beneath his feet into the steps of the gallows.

One could never have known from the eyes of the protagonist whether he was in truth the prince who was seeking his crown after the peregrinations of an unhappy life or a commoner of incredible daring. There he is, grave and taciturn: his head is bowed, the features of his face are pressed between the palms of his hands, and he is listening in silence to the words that, in strictest privacy, are addressed to him in a baroque speech by the former confessor of the king Don Sebastián, Fray Miguel de los Santos, who is at present promoting his cause. Let us hear what he says:

"You must realize, my lord," warns the insinuating voice of the old Augustinian, preacher to princes, "that although Your Majesty's miraculous return, after such a long and hopeless absence, is greatly desired, it is difficult to believe, and not without effort shall we succeed in seeing you restored to the throne. It is true that many of your faithful subjects, overshadowed, left behind, restricted to their homes since Portugal came under the Spanish Crown, dream only of the return of their long-lost king. It is true that the people, ever eager for marvels, seem ready to recognize him at any time in the person of whomsoever arrives well stocked with incredible and fantastic tales. But, in the face of this, we must on the other hand expect mistrust from the many who, if it did not suit their interest and convenience, would deny what they saw with their own eyes—all the more so, my lord, since the passing of time has caused the image of Don Sebastián to fade in their minds. And if the years, with their natural changes, allow for differences in his appearance—from the noble youth who disappeared in the sad Alcazarquivir expedition to the mature man who reappears today in Castilian lands—they also permit all sorts of doubts and nourish the hopes of all sorts of claims.

"Now that the prince Don Enrique is dead, there is no one, my lord, who can with authority recognize the king, save this poor old man speaking to you now. And my eyes, though clouded by age, rejoice on contemplating the return of their great and unfortunate penitent, of the poor king Don Sebastián, and they wish to bear witness to your being one and the same with that gallant youth. I have given assurances of that and sworn to it, not only to the Portuguese lords we are expecting tonight, but also, as I said before, to Doña Ana de Austria,* who, what with the impatience of her tender years and the seclusion of the convent, now burns with desire to receive the visit of the gentleman I have described to her as her royal cousin. Why was I to doubt my weakened vision? Identity, sire, is more a matter of the soul than of the body, and who could recognize better than I the soul that so many times bared itself before God through my mediation in the tribunal of penitence? May He grant that your extended absence, without depriving you of mettle, has taught you the prudence to control it, and even to conceal the prudence you've acquired, lest a display of that virtue, proving to be

*The daughter of Don Juan de Austria (1545–78), half-brother of Felipe II. Don Juan's military exploits included victories in the revolt of the Moriscos (see p. 4n) and the famous naval battle of Lepanto.

greater than that which could be expected from the natural maturing of your judgment, prevent people from recognizing in the overly prudent man that unrestrained and senseless youth who set off to lose all at Alcazarquivir. A terrible lesson, no doubt! But there is no lesson so great that it can change a person's character, and an excess of discretion would seem indiscreet in one famed for madness—in a king whose childhood would be satisfied with toys no smaller than armies and fleets; in one who tested his furor for war against Lisbon, which was the same as punishing his own body; in one who dreamed of conquering Hercules by breaking his pillars.* God grant, I say again, that the years and the adventures you have been through have tamed you without depriving you of the demeanor that befits your royal blood. A prince must always stand out, even in the midst of crowds and dressed in the humblest garments, for he bears royalty in his soul. He who has been born to reign walks toward the throne with the certainty of the stars, and there is no obstacle that can block his way, even though it might behoove him at times to evade them with cunning rather than assault them with courage, as is now the case.

"For, my lord, the difficulties hindering your just claim are now increased—a most vexing circumstance!—because several impostors have already tried to pass themselves off as the king Don Sebastián. May the fate of those luckless men not be visited upon your royal self! If such were to occur, who could ever state for sure in centuries to come that you were in truth the king? You yourself, sire, would perhaps suspect your blood of having deceived you, believing instead that you had had demons in your body. Only demons could have given such bad counsel to the impious hermit from Alcobaça, who began to

---

*Pillars of Hercules: the two promontories on either side of the Strait of Gibraltar; thus, the route to the Atlantic Ocean.

tell tall tales about the battle and his captivity, pretending to
be the lamented king so as to procure listeners and alms. A
lucky rascal, he lived by his deceit, and then he managed to
deceive death. His greed was punished in the galleys, and he
only found forgiveness from Heaven when it turned upon the
arrogance of the king Don Felipe, scattering with its fury the
Invincible Armada in which that miserable man was rowing.
A worse fate befell the other hermit, Mateo Alvarez, who
advanced the same claim shortly thereafter. His brain poisoned perhaps by the juices of the roots and grubs on which he
fed, the wretched man began to dream stories of Alcazarquivir. And no sooner had he invented them than he believed
them, and he made all those who listened to him believe
them. He furnished information about many youths and soldiers, and he knew about the death that had come to each,
and the where and the how, and what had become of those
who had been able to escape. And he explained what the
battle had been like, and by what hapless chance it had been
lost, and how Castilians and Portuguese and Andalusians had
fallen into the river in droves, and how a week later the river
still bore bloated corpses of men and horses. At first those who
stopped to listen were few, and they did so out of incredulous
curiosity. I myself went to hear him. He had a rasping, dry,
sharp voice. His blackened hands fluttered like birds, and his
voice sounded like their cawing. Later, his fame spread, and
people began to come from afar to ask him what had happened
to one relative or another who had never been heard from
since. The hermit would be silent for what seemed an eternity. No one dared breathe. Sometimes their hopes proved
vain: he would not say a word. But at other times he would
give the news they sought, and do so with details so vivid and
so plausible that they made his listeners turn pale and the
kinsmen burst into tears. It was also not unusual for him to

take the middle course between silence and specific information, responding with enigmas or parables, like the time he
chided a mother, reproaching her for her despair, and offered
her the example of a little beast: she should learn from the
family dog who, having seen the departing son off with a
puppy's leaps, now, old and blind and slow, stubbornly resisted death, which beckoned him from the dunghills and the
backwaters of the streams, in the hope of appearing, tearful
and dumb, before the missing man he had waited for beyond
the natural span of his life. 'The day that dog lies down to die
on the dungheap is the day you must give up hope for your
son's return,' he concluded. And the old woman fell on her
knees in the nettles and sobbed.

"Thus, my lord," Fray Miguel went on after a pause, "(and
permit me to enlarge upon these cases about which you perhaps have little knowledge, and whose details ought to be of
great interest to you), thus, I say, the hermit's reputation and
the number of his followers grew—until that terrible thing
occurred. When, from the depths of the silence in which they
were listening, there burst forth like a dry storm the cry pro-
claiming him king of Ericeira, and king of Portugal. When his
ears heard the cries that discovered beneath his rags the long-
lost Don Sebastián, the poor wretch felt the earth open beneath his feet. He raised his arms, he tried to speak. But no
sound came forth from his matted beard. He knew at that
moment that he would die. And when, four months later, he
was led to the gallows by order of the king's justice, one might
have said he was weeping with relief. May God forgive him!
He had not the strength for what was asked of him. That was
not meant for the shoulders of a frail hermit."

The friar stopped. And as his listener made not the slightest
movement, he concluded:

"My lord, if just one star were missing, the whole fabric of the firmament would collapse. Don Sebastián is missing from among the princes of the earth, and others have tried to fill his place until your arrival. But not one of them could bend Ulysses' bow, which awaits the strength of your arm. In you returns that wild young man who received from my hand so many times remission for his sins. If the peregrination that was his penance did not diminish his arrogance, it worked happy changes in his nature, at which my heart rejoices in secret, since secretly it knows what they are. For what man who had listened at that time to the anguished confessions of flesh tormented by its horror of flesh would not marvel at the serene virility that now shows in your eyes and is proclaimed by your actions? Make use of it, sire, to reclaim the throne and govern men!"

The friar lapsed into a weary silence after this exhortation. He was waiting. Then, the face that until that moment had been sunk in the hollow of his listener's hands detached itself from them and began to rise with deliberate vigor. Now its gaze glided loftily above the cleric's shining tonsure, his hoary locks, the fat nape of his neck. Fray Miguel had in the meanwhile sunk onto a chair, and there he had remained, limp as a marionette after the fair.

"Let's go, then!" he heard the king's rough voice command, denying him any rest.

He sprang from his seat and, with a mistrustful glance, after a brief hesitation, he directed his short, nimble steps toward the door. The gentleman's footsteps followed his own nervous footsteps through the gallery, as the hunter follows his dog.

When they came into Doña Ana's presence, the friar stepped aside and the gentleman advanced to the center of the room, so as to bow to her. The princess was waiting on her feet. From the border of her habit, which almost touched the ground, her slender figure stood erect and motionless. Only her hands, meeting to twist the sheerest of handkerchiefs, seemed in her to be uneasy. The man's eyes rose slowly, until they reached the lady's face. They found there a pair of delicate lips that, pressed together, almost disappeared into a colorless line; they lingered on her young features, still not clearly defined; they discovered two large, very serious eyes; and, at last, his gaze met hers. But it could hold it only a moment; for, with a blinking of lids, her gaze slid down the man's face to his beard, dropped at once, and, when on the ground, fastened upon the visitor's dusty boots.

It was Fray Miguel de los Santos who broke the silence.

"My lady," he said, "here, after so long a time, is your cousin, the king Don Sebastián of Portugal, about whose fate we have spoken so often. This secret visit, destined to have such public and solemn consequences, will bind that fate to your own. For, my lord," he added, now addressing the gentleman, "Your Majesty knows Doña Ana de Austria's feelings toward our just cause: none other than those which could be expected of so high a princess, daughter of the illustrious captain whose exploits have generously magnified the very king who succeeded you in your own lifetime."

"Do not take my silence as discourtesy, noble lady. Attribute it, rather, to my soul's astonishment at seeing you. For when this good Fray Miguel, for reasons of state, asked my consent to arrange our betrothal, I could not imagine such consummate beauty as the pawn of a political alliance. May I be forgiven, then, my happy discomposure in your presence."

"Leave off such gallantry, my lord. Do not think yourself obliged to use courtly flattery of the sort with me," she answered. Then, after a pause, she lent softness and gravity to her voice and went on: "This is the first time I've seen you, my lord Don Sebastián, and already I feel that our friendship

is old, to the point of not knowing where it springs from
(perhaps, I think, because its origin lies in our common blood,
and antedates the two of us). I have heard your ill-fated adventure recounted so often, your destiny is so familiar to me,
that if anything can overwhelm me in your presence it is to
have before my eyes, in flesh and blood, a figure of legend.
The story of the king Don Sebastián was almost a legendary
one for me. Before I was born you had already reigned, and
they had already given you up for lost. Whenever one of my
ladies-in-waiting related something about you (some tiny detail, anything other than the terrible event), I would ask her
in amazement, 'But, tell me, did you meet him? Did you see
him with your own eyes?' Now it is my eyes that can see—that
are seeing—Don Sebastián, and not as the unlucky hero of
Alcazarquivir, but as a gentleman who comes to me using
gallantry, and who asks me for help. This is something miraculous, a true portent. It is almost as if the king Don Rodrigo* had suddenly appeared before me, asking my help to
reconquer his realm."

"Your comparison with the king who lost Spain proves
painful to me, gentle princess. Painful, but just. For my misfortune imitated, in fact, that of the last of the Goths—
though I hope to recover from it with the hand Your Highness
deigns to offer me, so that mine will be less dire a fate."

"Pray excuse as imprudence on my part the unintended
offense implied in that comparison. In my mind, desire had
anticipated your successful restoration to the throne and, forgetting our present trials, I did not foresee that you might be
wounded by the memory of that other king who fatally succumbed in circumstances much like these. I merely wished to

*The last of the Visigoth kings of Spain, defeated in 711 by the Moslems,
who invaded the peninsula from North Africa that year and quickly dominated most of it.

describe to you my soul's joyous surprise seeing a hero appear again who had been given up for dead before I was born. But how could you understand this from your own life, which is single and continuous despite its many crises, first in its brilliant course, next in captivity, then in its peregrination? You would have to realize that this final dark and secret part spans all the years of my life."

She fell silent for a moment. Then she repeated: "All the years of my life!" Lost in wonder, the princess shook her head. Her hands, now quiet, rose up to her brow and the tips of her fingers passed slowly across her temples. At once, as if talking to herself, she murmured, "How many years, and how many sufferings, worries, and troubles! Can there have been any other king with such a wealth of experiences? And to think that Your Majesty, sire, who was already a king in his mother's womb, a king before he was a man, only to suffer thereafter all the misfortunes of men—to think, my lord, that you might have led a worthy and tranquil existence, like that of our Don Felipe, who used your loss for the peaceful increase of his grandeur. Then, indeed, you would have certainly had my esteem, my love as a kinswoman—never this heartfelt sharing in your destiny, which moves me so far as to wish to join with it in this time of misfortune."

"Being in your presence makes me feel that I have reached the end of my troubles. So let us look back on them no more, my lady. There will be time enough to retrace together the long and bitter odyssey of my life, about which, in any case, you have already been informed, as I understand, by Fray Miguel de los Santos. This is rather a time for providing the means to bring these troubles to an end, so that, recovering my lawful rights, rich in the experience I've acquired and poor in the lifetime I've wasted, I may again occupy that place where once my lack of experience all but deprived me of my life."

"Certainly, Don Sebastián. And now it is your discretion that instructs my carelessness. Forgive me if, troubled and confused in my happiness at being able to be of use to you, I forgot for a moment what matters most and, thinking only of the dangers you have undergone, lost sight of those that face you now, and of the ones still remaining until our enterprise is crowned."

"It is as good as crowned, in fact, if we may count upon your help. Your Highness' intervention promises good fortune."

"None will be so good to me as that of serving Your Majesty; and if the risks you run make me uneasy now, so much greater will be my reward when I see you restored to your rightful splendor."

"It will also be yours, my lady, by this act of your generosity. The act of restoring a deposed king to his throne is worthy indeed of the daughter of that captain who won such glorious battles on behalf of a monarch more given to the cares of an office clerk than to the dangers of war.* The daughter of Don Juan de Austria was born for the throne, and not to govern a community of nuns. And were I not loath to offer what is not yet mine, I would ask you at once to be my queen of Portugal."

"To secure the realm is what matters now. Need I remind you of that just as you reminded me a moment ago? So, my lord, look to what I must do. Command, and I shall obey you."

"I shall obey you," she had said. "Look to what I must do." The gentleman seemed puzzled; he was silent. The absolute peace of that room, with its floor of large black and white tiles, its chest of drawers, and the ivory crucifix on the wall above, had invaded his soul, and he was silent. . . . But fi-

---

*Felipe II, grandson of Fernando and Isabel, and king of Spain from 1556 to 1598, was known for his prudence. He was a bureaucratic ruler who devoted long hours to paperwork and directed the military campaigns from his office.

nally he had to come forth with a reply: she was to do nothing for the moment, but wait for events to unfold. To make frequent visits would be risky, and unnecessary besides, since "our good confessor" would take charge of keeping them in touch, as he had up to the present. Wasn't that so, father?—It was. Fray Miguel assented with a nod.

"Well then . . . !"

And sensing something between exasperation and forsakenness in the tone with which Doña Ana, while pretending to end the interview, was asking for directions with these words, the friar came forward from the corner where he had remained up to that point and explained to the princess in brief and persuasive terms something of what was planned. That very night they were expecting five Portuguese gentlemen who, as the foremost among the nobility of their country, were coming to recognize the king. Once they had sworn obedience to him, they would be the ones to prepare the uprising in the realm and the enthronement of Don Sebastián, so that the king of Spain, Don Felipe, would find himself faced with a fait accompli and with no other recourse but to recognize the man whose path he might otherwise have obstructed.

And since Doña Ana seemed surprised at this suspicion, unable to believe in such wickedness, the friar concluded:

"My lady, your tender years, the greatness of your birth, and the generosity of your heart combine to make you ignorant of the strong resistance of those interests that, in a highly intricate web, always oppose any change that threatens to disturb them, however much it be endorsed by justice and recommended by the public good. Your Highness must not expect the rights of the king Don Sebastián to make their way simply by being declared. On the contrary, they will have to take winding paths, devious byways, and slip in with subtle cunning so as to later break through by force." And after a pause and a rapid, furtive

glance at the princess' troubled face, he added: "The worry—
though a paltry one—that now seizes our spirits and checks our
movements is, my dear Doña Ana—it shames me to say it!—
the scarcity of resources upon which we can count to take care
of the inevitable expenses of the plot: emissaries, messages,
spies, and various other preparations and precautions."

The lady, who had listened somewhat distractedly, came to
herself with a sigh and said:

"I leave it all to your discretion, father. Trouble my spirit
no more, confused as it is by this grave matter and trusting
only in the authority of my confessor." And laying hold of a
small purse of blue velvet, she drew forth a handful of jewels
and offered them to the pretender.

"Here, dear cousin, take this gold, and let it be a token of
my faith in your right and my confidence in your person."

She also took a ring from her finger and placed it on the
little heap of chains, seals, and royal coats of arms that spar-
kled and winked diabolically from the hollow formed by the
joined palms of his strong hands. With all his vital spirits, all
the heat of his veins concentrated there, the man, grown
pale, felt that he was touching for the first time the metal of
his royal state; but the inexpressible pleasure at feeling himself
a king was tinged with the subtle suspicion of some sort of
fraud that partly defeated it.

Yet, in the face of the dubious charm of that power whose
symbol he was receiving, there loomed, so imposing that it
left him speechless, the great and pure truth of the maiden
who, in a tender impulse, had surrendered her jewels to him
and, with her jewels, her own destiny.

He bowed low, and left.

He left full of new strength, driven by the unconquerable
virtue of that talisman which made his spirit overflow. Fray

Miguel de los Santos, overwhelmed, watched him grow larger before his eyes with that impetuous majesty he knew so well: the same majesty that, twenty years before, had been the ruin of his young penitent, and whose terrifying strength he would have never suspected in the taciturn protégé who now, with this majesty, revealed himself as the truth of his own lie. So the friar submitted, without a word, to the imperious tone of his voice, which demanded compliance. When he realized he was losing his grip on the reins and was hopelessly entangled in the intrigue that he himself had contrived, he did not even try to resist: he submitted to his authority. And when, at nightfall, he had to lead the Portuguese noblemen coming to bring Don Sebastián's crown to the inn where the new king was waiting for them, he did not have the courage to attend the meeting. He ushered them into the room and stayed to listen behind the half-closed door. The murmurs reaching his ear from the other side fed the anguish of his heart and governed his pulse. His breath stopped short when, after a while, he heard the royal voice swell above the turbid sound of half-understood phrases, and exclaim with an angry and urgent calm:

"Look at me well. Look at me from head to toe. Listen to my voice. Study me as long as you like. And then tell me: Who am I? Tell me: Am I perhaps a false king, an impostor? If that's what you think, my lords, shout it to my face. Quickly, without hesitation—shout it! Open the windows, wake the neighbors, call all the people and point at me, charging: 'This man is an impostor who, by taking the realm of Portugal away from the great Felipe II, wishes to pass himself off as our king. This man is a liar who, filled with mad audacity, dares appear as the king Don Sebastián before us—his friends, his companions, who used to see him every day, who shared his table, who seconded him in his trials—seeking to impose his audac-

ity upon our stupefaction and force us to recognize him!'
Quickly! Heap infamy upon me if your souls harbor the slightest doubt! But quickly, tell me, my lords: Who am I?"

Mustering all his strength, Fray Miguel de los Santos rushed
into the room on hearing the cry of the king, who waited
now, his beard clasped in his left hand and his elbow cradled
in the right.

The Portuguese noblemen, taken aback and intimidated,
exchanged irresolute glances with an uneasiness that the
flickering light of the candles magnified into grimaces, while
the friar, full of anguish, followed the silent deliberations in
their faces. On behalf of all, the chief man among them
replied at last:

"My lord, you are the king," he said.

"I want to hear it from the lips of every one of you."

"You are the king, sire," repeated the others.

"In that case, my friends, why do your lips not speak my
name? Have they perhaps forgotten it?"

"The king Don Sebastián, my lord. I recognize you to be
the king Don Sebastián," proclaimed the man who had first
spoken, bending the knee before him and taking his hand. He
gave it to him to kiss.

Reassured, the friar now dared intervene:

"Sire," he suggested, "no doubt these gentlemen would like
to have the pleasure of embracing Your Majesty, in whom
they recover not only a king but a friend."

That night Fray Miguel had not yet calmed his heartbeat
through sleep when, just about daybreak, he received a message from Doña Ana, who was asking for her confessor. He
went to her in anxious haste.

"Here I am, my lady, at your command. What can possibly
have happened overnight to require my visit before that of

dawn?" And while he questioned her thus with a gallant smile, his eyes, uneasy, pressed for a swift reply.

But on seeing him, she seemed to have lost all reason for urgency, to be confused; and she searched for words in the folds of her lap. When she had sorted them out, she put an end to the pause:

"Forgive me, father, if in my sleeplessness I forgot your years and shortened your rest with my summons. Let this be my excuse: the hours of the night, drawn out and prolonged, have twisted my conscience into so cruel a knot that its pain, greater than my piety, marred the balm of prayers with which, time and again, I sought to soften it and made meaningless the holy words my lips were trying to pronounce. There was room in my breast for nothing but the torment of this doubt: whether what I am doing is indeed well done, and whether this matter of the king Don Sebastián is in accordance with God's will. I have gone over your words a thousand times, Father Miguel, and it even seemed to me that I was hearing them anew, in their soft persuasion, close to my pillow. But why is it, my father, that your counsel, which has always governed my conscience, has no power to assuage it now? In every act of my life I have always heeded your advice, and not even I understand my soul the way its old spiritual director does. Why, on this occasion, while so joyfully wishing to follow your pious guidance, does it feel insecure and tormented, unable to satisfy itself about the reasons that recommend to it what it so longs for? Whence my delight? Whence my affliction? Why do I tremble so in the presence of what I desire?

"Father Miguel, forgive me for having made you come in such a hurry. Your early rising is sleeplessness for me; your haste, my delay. I have sent for you, as my confessor, in my agony of soul. Already I know the meaning of that indulgent smile. I know full well how much you've done to reassure me, to set my spirit at ease. I know it well. But talk to me, talk to me about Don Sebastián! Tell me, how can I be sure? How will I know! You are his confessor; you were lucky enough to know his innermost thoughts, as you know mine, when he was just my age and had not yet been mistreated by adversity. And then, you have talked with him endlessly and have heard the story of his misfortunes. Don't be impatient, father. It's true that you have related that story to me and have patiently answered all my questions, however minute or silly they might have been. But try to understand, I myself have spoken with him only a few minutes, and have heard nothing from his lips but ceremonious phrases, a hollow shell of all I know of him from what you've told me. And as I've learned nothing more from him . . . Remember, father, that I am a princess, and I have a right to know, I have a right to be sure. I want to know, beyond a doubt, that he is indeed the king Don Sebastián. How can I be sure of it? Oh, father! I should like to follow in his footsteps. Not just where they lead now—I want to be able to go back in time with him, on his adventures in Europe, till I have made each of his hardships my own, and I want to be with him in captivity. And more, I would like to go back with him to the palace in Lisbon, when, full of enthusiasm, he was preparing the expedition that was to be his ruin. . . . But I'm raving, my father. That smile from the cold summit of your age tells me so. Yes, all my years put together do not reach back to such far-off times. But may not knowledge go back beyond the reach of memory, and is not all eternity present in one breath of a single soul? When we clasp his hands, we can touch the past created by his hands. To know, to be sure is what I ask. If only I could get inside his thoughts. . . . It's in the beating of his heart that his royal spirit will be known! If it is he, as he seems to be and as I believe, he can harbor no deceit, no evil. There can only be nobility in his breast, and his mouth can speak only truth."

While anxieties such as these were afflicting Doña Ana, and Fray Miguel was trying to calm her troubled heart, the man who was their cause was plunging from the proud crest of his aspirations to the darkness of a dungeon. That very night they had gone to arrest him at the inn, with officers of the law, on charges of imposture, and they took down his first deposition. After that, the judicial proceedings were begun at once, and four days later he was under sentence of death for treason. Although no confession could be wrung from him, it is on record in the final decree that the man who dared to pass himself off as the king Don Sebastián was in fact a pastrycook from the town of Madrigal, known there by the name of Gabriel Espinosa.

The time came for the sentence to be carried out, and, refusing all company, he chose to wait alone. He wanted to be alone with himself. Alone he passed the night. The night passed; the hour struck; footsteps were heard without, the stairs creaked, a bolt clattered, the door groaned, and the narrow cell was filled with men. They bound his hands, they took him down to the prison gate, they put him on the back of a mule, and, under heavy guard, he went forward through the crowd as if suspended in the air, slowly, stiff and swaying on his mount, like a solemn masker in the crush of carnival, preceded by the roll of the town crier's drum.

Then the procession entered the town square and, making its way through the people, slowly approached the gallows. Now everything happened with dreamlike slowness. And the convicted man, dragging his feet, had already climbed the steps of the scaffold, when a flurry of excitement stirred the square. What was it? What was going on? What breath from what gigantic lung had blown over the heads of the crowd? "It's his mother, she's coming!" was heard again and again. As if through the air, the mother of the pastrycook Gabrielillo Espinosa had been brought from Madrigal. Hidden in the rear of her house, she had not wanted to know anything about it. But a group of villagers, half-sympathetic, half-brutal, had gone to pull her from her lair so that she might witness the funeral rites of a king. And the old woman, wrapped in her widow's cloak, had allowed herself to be led without resistance. Now she was seen, looking stupidly out of a window that faced the scaffold.

"It's his mother!" they explained everywhere; and after the oft-repeated murmur, silence once more. The condemned man raised his eyes toward the window and made a strange grimace. Some thought it a cynical sneer; others, a look of pain; while still others thought they saw in it who knows what dark message. At last, a sentence issued from his lips. He said, as though speaking to himself: "Poor Don Sebastián, what an end you've come to!"

The rest was all very quick. With the bated breath of those who watch a falcon swoop down on its prey and, grasping it, hesitate a moment in space, so the people saw the hangman dangle in the air, grasping the convict. But when he had released him, and left that limp rag doll hanging from the gallows, one might have said that the entire scene had been nothing but a bad farce staged by some rustic players.

❦ The Bewitched

After having petitioned in vain at Court, the *indio** González Lobo—who had arrived in Spain toward the end of 1679 in the fleet of galleons whose cargo of gold went to pay for the king's wedding—retired to live in the city of Mérida, where one of his father's sisters made her home. Never again did González Lobo leave Mérida. Joyfully welcomed by his aunt Doña Luisa Alvarez, who had been left alone on being widowed shortly before, he helped her in the management of a small estate, which, years later, he would eventually inherit. It was there, then, that he spent the rest of his life. He divided his time between farming and prayer, and in the evenings he wrote. He wrote, along with many other documents, a lengthy description of his journey, in which, after innumerable digressions, he tells how he came into the presence of the Bewitched. It is to that account that this report refers.

Carlos II the Bewitched (1661–1700), last of the Hapsburg kings of Spain. His father, Felipe IV (1605–65), died when he was four. The degenerate product of generations of intermarriage and inbreeding, Carlos was a sickly, malformed person of subnormal intelligence. Impotent, he left no heir, and at his death the crown passed to the grandson of Louis XIV, the Bourbon king of France, setting off the War of the Spanish Succession (1702–13).

*Indian; son of a Spaniard and a native American.

91

It is not the draft of a solicitation, nor anything of the sort; it does not seem designed to establish or support any claim. It might best be characterized as a chronicle of his disappointment. He composed it, no doubt, to while away the long, sleepness nights of an old age wholly turned toward the past and confined within the walls of memory, at a time when no emotion, not even curiosity, could be awakened by the echoes—muffled, moreover, when they reached his ear—of the civil war in which the Crown of the unfortunate Carlos, now dead, was being contested.

Some day this remarkable manuscript should be published. I would give the complete text if it were not so long, and so uneven in its parts: it is crammed with tedious data about the West Indies trade, with critical appraisals that might possibly be of interest to present-day historians and economists; it gives too much attention to a comparison—moreover, quite irrelevant—between farming in Peru and the state of agriculture in Andalusia and Extremadura; it abounds in trivial details; it wastes time on incredible minutiae and delights in pondering the most negligible point, while occasionally slipping in, with a casual allusion, some atrocity that has come to his notice or else some act of admirable distinction. In any case, it would not seem wise to publish such a misshapen document without retouching it somewhat and relieving it of the many impertinent excrescences that make it so difficult and unpleasant to read.

It is worth pointing out that once the reader, at the expense of considerable effort, has finished it, he is left with the feeling that, despite so much insistent detail, something has somehow been kept up the sleeve. Other persons acquainted with the text have borne out this impression of mine; and a friend who studied the manuscript after I had aroused his interest in it went so far as to add in his letter thanking me:

"More than once, on turning a page and raising my head, I thought I could see at the back, in the semidarkness of the archives, the jet-black stare of González Lobo masking his scorn in the blinking of his half-closed eyes." In truth the document proves to be inordinately disconcerting, and it is filled with problems. For example: What was its purpose? Why was it written? One can accept that it might have had no other purpose than to while away the solitary hours of an old man reduced to feeding on his memories. But how can one explain the fact that, after so much repetition, it never clearly says what, precisely, was the nature of the claim for favor that its author brought to the Court, nor what it was based on?

Furthermore: assuming that the said basis for a claim could only come to him through his father's line, it is astonishing that the latter is never once mentioned in the entire account. One could speculate that González Lobo might have lost his father at a very early age and, that being the case, would have very few memories of him. But in fact he even omits his name—while, on the other hand, overwhelming us with observations on the climate and flora, and tiring us with an inventory of the riches amassed in the cathedral church of Sigüenza. In any case, whatever information he gives us about his life prior to his voyage is extremely concise, and always brought up in an incidental way. We learn about the priest from whose hands he received sacraments and penances in an episode presented as an example to youth: he tells how the good friar, exasperated by the obstinacy with which his pupil resisted his reprimands in stubborn silence, threw the books to the floor, made the sign of the cross over him, and left him alone with Plutarch and Virgil. All this is mentioned by way of apology, or rather as a moralizing lament for the deficiencies of style that would no doubt mar his prose.

But that is not the only inexplicable thing in a narrative so laden with idle explanations. Together with problems of such magnitude can be found others that are more subtle. The arduous and protracted nature of the journey, the fact that the nearer he drew to the Court, the longer he stayed at each stopping place (in Seville alone the *indio* González stayed for more than three years, with no justification whatsoever in his memoirs for so prolonged a residence in a city where nothing should have detained him)—all this creates something of an enigma when contrasted with his sudden decision to drop his claims and leave Madrid, as soon as he had seen the king. And there are many such enigmas.

The narrative opens with the start of his voyage and closes with his visit to King Carlos II in a chamber of the palace. "As a token of his favor"—these are his final words—"His Majesty held out his hand to be kissed. But before I could take it a curious little monkey that had been playing nearby jumped upon it, and distracted His Highness' attention by demanding to be petted. Then I understood that it was time, and in respectful silence I withdrew."

Silent, too, is the initial scene of the manuscript, in which the *indio* González takes leave of his mother. There are no explanations, no tears. We see the two figures standing against the sky, in a landscape of Andean peaks, at the break of day. González has had to travel far to arrive there by dawn; and now, mother and son walk without speaking, side by side, toward the church, a little larger and a little less poor than the dwellings nearby. Together they hear mass. Once it is over, González resumes his descent along the cordilleran footpaths.

A little farther on, we find him amid the bustle of the port. There, his slight figure can scarcely be made out in the flurry of confusion, among the tangled web of comings and goings all around him. He stands still, waiting, absorbed in watching the preparation of the fleet, facing the shimmering, blinding ocean. On the ground beside him is a small chest. Everything whirls around his patient waiting: sailors, officials, stevedores, soldiers; shouts, orders, blows. The *indio* González Lobo has been standing quietly in the same spot for two hours, and yet another two or three will pass before the countless legs of the first galley begin to move in time, dragging its belly over the thick waters of the port. Then he will embark with his chest. As for the long voyage, his memoirs contain only this succinct allusion: "It was a good crossing."

But in the absence of incidents to record, and perhaps as a result of worrisome expectations that never came to pass, he fills up folio after folio explaining the obstacles, risks, and damages brought about by the many buccaneers that infest the seas, proposing remedies that could be adopted so as to avoid the heavy losses suffered on their account by the interests of the Crown. Anyone reading this would think it had been written, not by a traveler, but by a politician or perhaps some reforming *arbitrista:* * it is a mass of more or less well-founded lucubrations of questionable originality. He loses his way; he falls into generalities. And we do not meet him again until Seville.

In Seville we see him reemerge from a maze of moral, economic, and administrative reflections, following a black man who carries the chest on his shoulder and guides him through a maze of narrow streets in search of lodgings. He has left behind him the ship from which he disembarked. It is still there, swaying in the river; its masts, all pennants flying, can be seen close by. But between González Lobo, who is now following the black man with his chest, and the vessel that brought him from America, there lies the customhouse. In the

* A person who proposed absurd, farfetched solutions for the serious problems of that period.

entire document there is not one vehement expression, not a single gesture of impatience or complaining inflection: nothing disturbs the story's impassive course. But anyone who has grown familiar with his style, and has taken the pulse of his prose, and has learned to feel the throbbing that is hidden beneath the rhetoric then in use can detect, in his reflections on improved regulation of trade with the Indies and on some standards of good government whose adoption might possibly have been advisable, all the tedium of interminable proceedings capable of exasperating a person of less fine temper.

It would go beyond the purpose of these notes, intended only to draw attention to the curious manuscript, to offer here a complete summary of its contents. Perhaps someday it will be published with the scholarly care it deserves, duly annotated, and prefaced with a philological study in which the many questions raised by its style can be examined and clarified. For at the very first sight one notices that the author's prose, as well as his ideas, are anachronistic for the time. And I even think that it might be possible to differentiate in them notions, turns of phrase, and reactions corresponding to two, and perhaps more, strata; in short, to the attitudes and manners of different generations, including ones previous to his own—all of which would be understandable given González Lobo's personal circumstances. At the same time, and as usually occurs, the results of this mixture remind one of contemporary sensibilities.

Such a study has yet to be made; and without its guidance it would seem inadvisable to publish a book of this sort, which would also have to be prefaced with a geographical-chronological table tracing the itinerary of his journey—in and of itself no small task, considering the great confusion and disorder with which, in its pages, facts are scrambled, dates altered, and events repeated, and eyewitness accounts are mixed with hearsay, things past with things present, events with judgments, and personal opinion with that of others.

For the moment, I wish to limit myself to anticipating this bibliographical note by again calling attention to the main problem posed by the work: that is, what was the true purpose of a journey whose motives are most obscure, if not intentionally obscured, and what relationship could there have been between the said purpose and his subsequent writing of the account? I must confess that, in my preoccupation, I have toyed with several hypotheses, quickly cast aside, however, as unsatisfactory. After turning it over and over in my mind, I discarded as too fantastic and totally unfounded the supposition that the *indio* González Lobo may have been concealing an identity by which he might have felt himself called to some high destiny, as a descendant, for example, of who knows what noble lineage. At bottom, that would hardly clarify anything. It also occurred to me to wonder whether his work might be a mere literary invention, carefully worked out in all its seeming negligence to symbolize the uneven and unforeseeable course of human life, implicitly moralizing upon the vanity of all the pursuits in which existence is spent. For several weeks I held enthusiastically to this interpretation, according to which the protagonist might even be an imaginary character. But in the last analysis I had to resign myself to discarding it: the literary consciousness of the period would surely have expressed such an idea in quite a different way.

However, this is not the moment to elaborate on such questions, but rather to describe the manuscript and briefly summarize its contents.

There is a passage—a long, interminable passage—in which González Lobo appears lost in the maze of the Court. He describes with pitiless exactitude his comings and goings through the labyrinth of corridors and antechambers, where hope is lost and one can see the turns of time. He insists on setting down each step he took, without omitting a single one. Page after page is filled with annoying references and details of absolutely no importance, and it is hard to imagine why they are included. Page after page is filled with paragraphs like this: "I went in, this time without a hitch, thanks to the fact that I was already quite familiar to the head of the conciergerie; but at the foot of the great stairway that begins in the vestibule"—he is referring to the palace of the Council of the Indies, * the scene of many of his efforts—"I found that the guard had changed. I was thus forced to again explain my entire business as on previous days, and to wait for a page to go up and inquire whether I might be admitted. While waiting, I passed the time looking at the people moving up and down the stairs: gentlemen and clerics who were bowing to one another, who were stopping to talk or were moving forward between bows. My good page took some time before returning with the message that I would be received by the fifth clerk of the Third Secretariat, who was qualified to hear my business. I followed an orderly upstairs, and I took a seat in the antechamber of the worthy clerk. It was the same antechamber where I had to wait on the first day, and I sat down on the same bench where I had then waited more than an hour and a half. Nor did the wait promise to be brief on this occasion either. Time went by; I saw the door open and close an infinite number of times, and on several occasions I saw the fifth clerk himself go in and out, passing by my side without a hint of having seen me, frowning and with his eyes straight ahead. Finally, tired of waiting, I approached the orderly at the door

*A royal council established in 1524 to supervise the Spanish possessions in America.

to remind him of my case. The good man recommended patience; but, so that I might not lose it altogether, he decided to let me go farther in, and he left me in the very office of the worthy clerk, who would soon be returning to his desk. While waiting for him to appear, I wondered if he would remember my business, and if perhaps he would not refer me, as he had the time before, to the Secretariat of another Section of the Royal Council. There was a pile of dockets on top of his desk, and the walls of the room were covered with bookshelves, also filled with folders. In the front of the chamber, over the back of the worthy clerk's armchair, hung a large and not very good portrait of the late king Don Felipe IV. On a chair near the table, another pile of dockets was awaiting its turn. Open, full of thick ink, the tin inkwell was also waiting for the worthy fifth clerk of the Secretariat. . . . But that morning it was impossible for me to talk with him, because he entered at last, greatly agitated, in search of a dossier, and he begged me with all courtesy to be so kind as to excuse him, for he had some business with His Lordship and was not free to hear me at that moment."

Tirelessly, the *indio* González dilutes his story with similar particulars, omitting neither day nor hour, to the point of frequently repeating two, three, and even more times, in almost the same words, his account of identical efforts, in such a way that they can only be distinguished by their date. And when the reader thinks he has arrived at the end of an extremely arduous day, he sees unfolding before his tired eyes a similar one, which he will also have to go through step by step, only to reach the next day. The author might well have avoided the labor—and spared his readers from it as well—by merely writing down, if it was so important to his intention, the number of visits he had to make to a particular office, and on what dates. Why did he not do so? Did he perhaps derive some strange pleasure from watching the manuscript unfold beneath his pen with the shapeless growth of a tumor and seeing its volume increase to the point of threatening to make the narrative itself equal in length to the amount of time it covers? What need had we to know, were that not the case, that there were forty-six steps in the stairway of the palace of the Holy Office, * and how many windows lined each of its facades?

Anyone who carries out faithfully the self-imposed task of going through the entire manuscript, from beginning to end, line by line, and without skipping a single point, experiences not relief but real emotion when, along the way, its direction takes an entirely unforeseen turn, opening up new perspectives to a mind all but overcome by boredom. "The next day, Sunday, I went to Dr. Curtius for confession," one reads with no transition whatsoever. The sentence bursts forth from the monotonous text like a sudden flash in dull, gray sand. . . . But if the tender tremor radiated by that word *confession* has momentarily raised a hope that the story might open up into intimate vibrations, it only goes to show how, on the contrary, the outer shell of his twisted constraints will now be sanctioned by the secrecy of the sacrament. Always prodigal with details, the author keeps silent about what is most important. The scene has changed, but not the attitude. We see the slight form of González Lobo advance, go slowly up the middle of the wide stone steps toward the portico of the church; we see him pause for a moment, off to one side, take a coin from his purse, and give alms to a beggar. Still more: we are informed with idle exactitude that the beggar is a blind, paralytic old man whose limbs are tightly bound in hard, shapeless bandages. And González adds yet another long digression,

---

*The Inquisition.

regretting that he has not sufficient means to alleviate the misery of the rest of the poor installed, like a fringe of decay, all along the steps.

At last the *indio's* figure fades into the hollow of the atrium. He has lifted the heavy curtain; he has entered the nave; he has genuflected deeply before the high altar. Then he approaches the confessional. Near it he waits, kneeling, for his turn to come. How many times have the beads of his rosary passed through his fingertips when, at last, a fat white hand beckons him from the dark to approach the confessional? González Lobo records the fleeting gesture of that hand shining white in the shadows. He has also retained through the years the impression of unpleasant harshness caused in his ear by his confessor's Teutonic inflections and, long after, he takes pleasure in recording this as well. But that is all. "I kissed his hand, and I went to hear holy mass near a column."

It is disconcerting—disconcerting and somewhat irritating—to see how, after demonstrating such reserve, he then proceeds to ponder the solemnity of the mass: the heart-rending purity of the youthful voices that, from the choir, responded to the grave Latin words from the altar "as though the heavens had opened and angels were singing the glory of the Resurrected Christ." The liturgical phrases and chants, the shine of the silver and the gold, the myriad lights, and the dense volutes of incense ascending before the altarpiece between twisted columns, covered with ivy, toward the small broken pediments—all that was no greater novelty than it is today, nor did it call for special mention. Only with difficulty would we convince ourselves that the author has not lingered over these details so as to cover up his omission of what concerns him personally and to fill by means of this device the hiatus between his confession—in which doubtless some profane subject matter was introduced—and the visit he made on the following morning, invoking Dr. Curtius' name, to the residence of the Society of Jesus. * "I pulled the bell," he says, when he has led us up to the door, "and heard it ring closer and louder than I had expected."

It is, once again, a succinct reference to an insignificant fact. But behind it the reader, by now exhausted, would like to divine a scene charged with tension: he pictures to himself again the lean, sallow figure of González Lobo, who approaches the door of the residence with his customary slowness, his sad, slow, impassive air, and, upon reaching it, slowly lifts his hand up to the bellpull. But that fine, long, languid hand grasps it and pulls at it with a violent jerk, and then releases it again at once. Now, while the bellpull swings before his indifferent eyes, he observes that the bell was too close by and that it has rung too loudly.

But, in truth, he says nothing of this. He says, "I pulled the bell, and heard it ring closer and louder than I had expected. Its din had scarcely subsided when I heard the steps of the porter, who was coming to open the door for me, and who, on learning my name, let me come in at once." In his company, the reader enters a room where González will wait, standing by the table. In the room there is nothing but that small table, placed in the center, a couple of chairs, and a cabinet set against the wall, with a great crucifix above. The wait is long. Its outcome is this: "I was not able to see the Inquisitor General in person. But, in his name, I was referred to the house of Baroness von Berlips, the same lady known by the common people under the nickname of 'The Partridge,' who, as they assured me, would have full information about my case when I got there. But I soon ascertained," he adds, "that to be re-

---

*Religious order founded by St. Ignatius of Loyola in 1534 to carry out the ecclesiastical policy of the Counter Reformation.

ceived by her would be no simple matter. The power of magnates is measured by the number of petitioners who knock at their doors, and there the whole courtyard of the house was an antechamber."

In a leap, the narrative transports us from the Jesuit residence—so silent that the loud ringing of a bell can fall in its vestibule like a stone in a well—to an old palace in whose courtyard is assembled a bustling swarm of suppliants, busy trafficking in influence, applications for exemptions, the purchase of positions, petitions of grace, or the procurement of privileges. "I stationed myself at a turn of the gallery and was whiling away the long wait by contemplating the great variety of appearances and conditions converging there, when a soldier, placing his hand on my shoulder, asked me where I had come from and for what purpose. Before I could answer, he hastened to apologize for his curiosity, adding that the long wait was an invitation to pass the time in some way, and the memory of one's homeland is always a pleasant topic of conversation. For his part, he told me he was a native of Flanders and that he was at present serving in the guard of the Royal Palace, in hopes of later securing a position as gardener in its dependencies; that this hope was founded on and supported by the influence of his wife, who was the king's dwarf and who had already given more than one indication of her skill in obtaining small favors. It occurred to me then, while I was listening to him, that that might be a good shortcut to reach my desired goal more quickly; and so, I told him that the latter was none other than to kiss His Majesty's feet, but that, being a stranger at the Court and without friends, I could find no way to reach his royal person. My inspiration," he adds, "proved to be a happy one, for, coming close to my ear, and after describing at great length his utmost sympathy for my helpless situation and his desire to serve me, he ended by saying that perhaps his aforementioned wife—who was, as he had told me, the dwarf Doña Antoñita Núñez, of the King's Chamber—could arrange some way to introduce me into his august presence, and that she would no doubt be willing to do so, assuming that I knew how to ingratiate myself with her and prevail upon her goodwill with the gift of the ring he saw on my little finger."

The pages immediately following are, in my opinion, those of greatest literary interest in the manuscript. Not so much for their style, which invariably maintains all its characteristics: a touch of archaism, occasional clumsy haste, and always that elusive manner in which at times one thinks one can identify the circumlocutions of official prose, and at other times the assumptions of a person writing for his own enjoyment, with no thought of any possible readers—not so much for their style as for their composition, with which González Lobo seems to have taken great pains. The narrative swells at this point, it loses its habitual dryness, and it even seems to dance with flashes of unwonted good humor. González takes pleasure in describing the appearance and mannerisms of Doña Antoñita, her words and her silences, during the course of the curious negotiation.

If these pages had not already gone beyond the limits of what is prudent, I would reproduce the passage in its entirety. But discretion obliges me to limit myself to a sampling of its nature. "At this point," he writes, "she dropped her handkerchief and waited, looking at me, for me to pick it up. As I bent down to get it, I saw her little eyes laughing on a level with my head. She took the handkerchief I returned to her and crumpled it between the tiny fingers of a hand already adorned with my ring. She thanked me, and her laugh sounded like a flageolet. Her eyes faded, and now, their brilliance extinguished, her enormous forehead was hard and cold as stone."

No doubt we are witnessing yet another display of minute detail. But is one not aware of a note of amusement here, which, in so apathetic a writer, seems to be the result of the elation felt by someone who, at last, unexpectedly, has found the way out of the maze where he has been lost and is preparing to leave it without haste? His worries have disappeared, and perhaps he enjoys lingering in the very place from which he was so eager to escape before.

From here on, the narrative loses its habitual heaviness and, as though responding to the rhythm of his heart, speeds up without breaking stride. He bears the weight of his wearisome voyage, and the countless folios that contain its events, from the distant mass celebrated in the Andean peaks until this moment in which he is about to appear before His Catholic Majesty, seem to embrace all the experiences of a lifetime.

And now we see the *indio* González Lobo in the company of the dwarf, Doña Antoñita, on the way to the Alcazar. Always at her side, he passes through courtyards, iron gates, vestibules, guards, corridors, antechambers. Behind him lay the Plaza de Armas,* where a squadron of cavalry was maneuvering; behind him lay the smooth marble stairway; behind him lay the wide gallery, opening onto a courtyard on the right, and the wall on the left decorated with the painting of a famous battle, which he did not stop to look at, but of which his memory kept the image of thickly massed companies of a tercio† that, from a well-defined perspective, was moving in echelons of twisted files toward the lofty, enclosed, defended citadel. . . . And now the enormous doorway, whose two oak

* A parade ground.
† A Spanish infantry regiment in the sixteenth and seventeenth centuries.

panels had opened before them when they reached the top of the stairs, closed again behind them. The carpets silenced their footsteps, imposing circumspection, and the mirrors led them forward toward the depths of desolate halls sunk in shadow.

Doña Antoñita's hand crept up to the handle of a gleaming door, and her soft fingers stuck to the shiny metal of the knob, making it turn without a sound. Then, suddenly, González Lobo found himself before the king.

"His Majesty," he tells us, "was seated in an enormous armchair on a dais, and his feet rested on a cushion of to-bacco-colored silk placed atop a footstool. At his side lay a small white dog." He describes—and it is astonishing how in so short a time he could have taken it all in the way he did, and kept it in his memory—everything from the king's thin, drooping legs to his lank, colorless hair. He informs us that the Mechlin lace adorning his chest was soaked with the endless slobber flowing from his lips. He lets us know that the buckles on his shoes were of silver, that his apparel was of black velvet. "The rich attire in which His Majesty was dressed," González writes, "gave off a strong stench of urine; later I learned of the incontinence he suffered from." With the same unshakable simplicity he goes on for three folios listing all the details that his incredible memory retained about the chamber and the manner in which it was furnished. Regarding the audience itself, which ought to have been, precisely, the most memorable thing for him, he sets down only these words, with which, in fact, he brings his lengthy manuscript to a close: "Seeing a stranger in the doorway, the little dog was startled, and His Majesty seemed troubled. But as soon as he saw the head of his dwarf, who was moving forward ahead of me, he recovered his composure. Doña Antoñita went up to him and spoke a few words in his ear. As a token of his favor, His Majesty held out his hand to be kissed. But before I could take it a curious little monkey that had been playing nearby jumped upon it, and distracted His Highness' attention by demanding to be petted. Then I understood that it was time, and in respectful silence I withdrew."

❧ The Inquisitor

Wbat joy! What excitement! What fireworks and music! The Grand Rabbi of the Jews, a man of consummate virtue and knowledge, having finally seen the light of truth, was bowing his head to the water of baptism. All the city joined in celebration.

On that unforgettable day, while giving thanks to Christ our Lord, within His Church at last, the former rabbi had only one reason to grieve. But it came from the very bottom of his heart: that his deceased wife, Rebeca, had been unable to take part in the blessing that he did share—fortunately—with Marta, their only daughter, and the other members of his household, all baptized with great solemnity in the same ceremony. That was his thorn, his secret sorrow on such a glorious day; that, and—something else—the dubious fate (more than dubious, fearful) of his ancestors, an illustrious line that he had revered in his grandfather and his father, generations of religious, learned, and good men who, however, after the

The persecutions of 1391 and 1412–14 created a new religious and social problem in Spain, that of *conversos* (converts) or New Christians. These were Jews who had been forced to convert to Christianity. The Inquisition was instituted to root out those converts who continued to practice Judaism in secret, many of whom had risen to important positions within Christian society. The failure of forced conversions prompted the expulsion of the Jews from Spain in 1492.

coming of the Messiah, had been incapable of recognizing Him and had clung for centuries to the old, invalidated Law.

The New Christian asked himself for what merits his soul and been accorded a grace denied to them, and by what design of Providence, now, after almost fifteen hundred years of stubborn, hardened, and deadly pride, it was he, there, in that small city of the Castilian plateau—he alone, of all his long lineage—who, after having presided over the venerable synagogue in an exemplary manner, was to take that scandalous and blessed step by means of which he was entering on the path of salvation. Before, quite some time before declaring himself a convert, he had devoted hours, long hours, countless hours, to studying in theological terms the enigma of such a destiny. He could not decipher it. He had to reject more than once as a sin of pride the only plausible answer that came to mind, and his meditations served but to persuade him that such a grace imposed burdens and made demands upon him in proportion to its singular magnitude, so that, at the least, he would have to justify it, a posteriori, by his actions. He understood clearly that he was beholden to Holy Church in a greater degree than other Christians. He took it for granted that his salvation would have to be the fruit of a most arduous effort on behalf of the Faith, and he resolved—as the sudden, happy result of his meditations—not to consider himself fulfilled until he had earned and achieved episcopal dignity right there, in the very city where he had held that of Grand Rabbi, becoming thus a marvel to all eyes and an example to all souls.

So he was ordained a priest, went to the Court, sojourned in Rome, and before eight years had passed his wisdom, his prudence, and his tireless effort finally earned him the miter of the diocese from whose episcopal see he would serve God until his death. His chosen path was full of rough and cragged steps—more, perhaps, than he could have imagined. But he did not succumb: it can even be said that he never hesitated for an instant. The present account deals with one of those moments of trial. We shall find the bishop on perhaps the most dreadful day of his life. There we have him, hard at work, almost at the break of day. He has had very little supper: scarcely a mouthful, without raising his eyes from his papers. Then, pushing the dishes to the far end of the table, away from the inkwell and the bundles of papers, he has immersed himself again in his work. At the far end of the table, clustered apart, are a large loaf of white bread with a crust missing, several plums on a plate, the remains of cold meat on another, a little jug of wine, an unopened jar of preserves. . . . Since it was late, His Excellency the bishop had dismissed his page, his secretary, everyone, and had served the meal himself. He liked it that way; many nights he would remain there until very late, without bothering a soul. But today it would have been hard to bear the presence of anyone; he needed to concentrate, without anyone disturbing him, on his study of the case. The very next day the Holy Tribunal was meeting under his presidency. Those wretches below were awaiting justice, and he was not a man to shirk or put off the fulfillment of his duties, nor to relinquish his own judgment to the opinions of others: he had always examined in detail every document, however minor, of every dossier; he had reviewed each proceeding, action, and piece of evidence until reaching a firm conviction upon which to base his uncompromising decision. Now, in this instance, he had everything gathered together before his eyes; it was all meticulously arranged and displayed, in folio after folio, from the very beginning, with the denunciation of the convert Antonio María Lucero, up to the drafts of the sentence to be decreed the following day against the entire group of Judaizers* implicated in the case. There was the record of the arrest of Lucero, surprised in his sleep and taken prisoner amid the fright and alarm of his household; the words he had let slip in that confused situation—rather ambiguous words, to be sure—were all set down. And then, his successive declarations over several months of interrogations, some of them interrupted by sighs and moans, screams and pleas for mercy under torture; it was all noted down and transcribed with scrupulous precision. In the course of the meticulous proceedings, in the innumerable, drawn-out steps that followed one after the other, Lucero had denied everything with maddening obstinacy. He had persisted even as they twisted his limbs on the rack. He denied everything while cursing, while imploring, while moaning. He denied everything always. However—someone else, perhaps, might not have noticed, but how could it possibly escape *him?*—the bishop was well aware that those invocations uttered by the accused in the confusion of his spirit, in darkness, pain, and fear, did indeed contain, at times, the holy name of God mingled with howls and threats; but not once did they appeal to Our Lord Jesus Christ, the Virgin, or the saints, to whom, nevertheless, he seemed so devoted under more tranquil circumstances. . . .

As he now reviewed the declarations obtained by means of torture—a proceeding that, for many reasons, the bishop had thought it his duty to witness at the time—he remembered with displeasure the look that Antonio María, hanging by his ankles, his head almost touching the ground, had directed at him from below. He knew very well what that look meant: it contained an allusion to the past, it was intended to recall the days when both of them, the accused man being subjected to

Conversos or New Christians who continued to practice Judaism in secret.

torture and his judge, the bishop and president of the Holy Tribunal, had still been Jews; to remind him of that occasion long ago when the goldsmith, then a slender, smiling youth, had respectfully approached his rabbi to ask for the hand of Sarah, the younger sister of Rebeca, still alive at the time, and the rabbi, after thinking about it, had found nothing against the marriage, and had himself officiated at the wedding of Lucero and his sister-in-law Sarah. Yes, that was what those eyes, shining near the ground in the darkness of the dungeon, forcing him to look away, were trying to remind him of; they were hoping for help from an old friendship and family tie entirely unrelated to the matter at issue. Thus that look was tantamount to an indecent wink of complicity, to an attempt at bribery. And it only served to furnish new evidence against him, for was it not meant to speak to and to move in the prelate who so zealously watched over the purity of the faith that erstwhile Jew, the Jew abjured by both?

Those people knew very well, or they imagined they did— the bishop now thought—what his weak point might be, and they had tried, with devious pertinacity, to approach him. Had they not attempted, from the very start—and what better proof of their guilty conscience, what more explicit confession of their lack of trust in the merciful justice of the Church!— had they not attempted to soften him through the mediation of Marta, his little daughter, an innocent child, involving her in this way? After so many months he felt again a surge of indignation that they had dared resort to what was most worthy of respect: the candor of the young. Absolved by her youth, Marta had appeared before her father to intercede on behalf of Antonio María Lucero, who had just been arrested on suspicion. It was not difficult to establish that she had done so at the urging of her childhood friend and—His Excellency frowned—first cousin, in fact, on her mother's side, Juanita

Lucero, who had, in turn, been coached no doubt by the Jewish relatives of her father, the convert Lucero, now sus- pected of Judaizing. On her knees, and with words she might well have rehearsed, the girl had implored the bishop. A diabolical temptation, for did Christ not say: *He that loveth son or daughter more than me is not worthy of me?*

His pen on high, and his myopic eyes staring absently at the shadowy wall of the room, the prelate allowed a sigh to slip from deep within his chest. He could not concentrate on the task; he could not prevent the flight of his imagination toward that only child, his pride and joy, that frail, silent, impetuous young girl who now, in her bedroom, lost to the world, sunk in the blissful abandonment of slumber, was sleeping quietly, while he kept watch, scratching at the silence of the night with his pen. She was—the bishop told himself—the last offspring of that old lineage whose most worthy name he had had to renounce so as to enter the mystical body of Christ, and whose final traces would be erased at last when, in time, she married—if indeed she was to marry—an Old Christian, * perhaps (why not?) of noble blood, and would then, faithful and reserved, industrious and cheerful, raise a new line of descendants in the heart of that house. With this longed-for prospect in mind, the bishop felt with renewed urgency the need to keep his daughter from any contact that might con- taminate her, free from entrapments, apart. And, recalling how they had tried to take advantage of the purity of her soul for the benefit of the accused Lucero, he felt anger rise in his throat, as though the painful scene had occurred only yester- day. He could see the child saying to him, as she kneeled at his feet: "Father, poor Antonio María is guilty of nothing. Father, I"—she! the innocent one!—"Father, I know very

---

*See p. 6n.

well that he's a good man. Save him!" Yes, save him. As if that—precisely that, to save those who have gone astray— were not the purpose of the Inquisition. Seizing her by the wrist, the bishop found out immediately how the whole plot had been contrived, how the whole web had been spun. The decoy was, clearly, the grief-stricken Juanita Lucero; and all the relatives, no doubt, had joined to stage the scene that, like a *coup de théâtre*, would—such was their aim—bend the dignitary's conscience with the subtle bribe of a child's tears. But it is written: *If thy right hand offend thee, cut it off, and cast it from thee.* As a preliminary measure and not as a punishment but rather out of precaution, the bishop ordered the child to remain in her room until further notice, while he himself retired to ponder the meaning and scope of that act: his daughter's appearing before him and, after kissing his ring and his hand, pleading with him on behalf of a Judaizer. And he concluded, to his amazement, shortly thereafter, that, despite all his care, he must have been guilty of some failure in Marta's education, since her imprudence had been so extreme.

He then decided to dismiss her tutor and catechist, that Dr. Bartolomé Pérez whom he had so carefully selected seven years before, and of whom it could be said, at the very least, that he had strayed into lenient ways, allowing his pupil free time for vain conversations and tolerating in her a state of mind disposed to take pleasure in such conversations with more feeling than good judgment.

The bishop needed many days to weigh and not entirely dismiss his scruples. Perhaps—he feared—distracted by the concerns of his diocese, he had allowed evil to invade his own household and a poisoned thorn to prick his flesh. With great rigor, he examined his conduct once again. Had he thoroughly fulfilled his duties as a father? The first thing he did when Our Lord decided to open his eyes to the truth and to open the doors of His Church to him was to seek out for that unfortunate babe, motherless from birth, not only nurses and maidservants of irreproachable faith, but also a tutor who would guarantee her Christian education. To separate her as far as possible from kinsfolk still too new in the Faith, to commend her to a man free from all suspicion in point of doctrine and conduct—such had been his design. The former rabbi sought out, selected, and summoned for such a delicate mission a learned and simple man, the same Dr. Bartolomé Pérez, the son, grandson, and great-grandson of farmers, a peasant who by dint of his own merit had raised himself from the small plot over which his ancestors had stooped, left the village, and at that time was serving, discreetly and humbly— after having distinguished himself in Scripture study—as co-adjutor in a parish that offered those in charge more work than it did rewards. It should be said that nothing about him pleased the illustrious convert as much as his plainness, his good sense, his easy peasant aplomb, all preserved beneath his cassock like an indestructible core of cheerful steadfastness. Before explaining his intentions, the bishop had three long conversations with him on matters of doctrine, and he found him to be learned without ostentation, a reasoner who did not quibble, a scholar who was neither flighty, anxious, nor troubled. On the lips of Dr. Bartolomé Pérez the most intricate subject became obvious, simple. And then, his clear, affectionate eyes promised the child the kind treatment and tenderness of heart already so familiar to the children of his poor parish. Dr. Pérez finally accepted the illustrious convert's proposal after together they had provided the old parish priest with another suitable coadjutor, and he went to live in that house where he rightfully hoped to gain in knowledge with no loss of charity. And, in fact, when his patron was invested with the bishopric, Dr. Pérez was granted the benefice of a canonry through his influence. Meanwhile, nothing but praise was heard for the religious education of the child, who obediently followed her teacher's guidance. But now . . . How was this to be explained, the bishop asked himself. What fault, what fissure did this recent development reveal in so careful, finished, and perfect a work? Might the evil not have lain precisely—he asked himself—in what he, perhaps in error, in haste, had thought to be the main advantage: in the self-confident and complacent certainty of the Old Christian, asleep in a routine of faith? And his suspicion seemed confirmed by the calm, placid, one might almost say approving air with which Dr. Pérez reacted to the news when the bishop summoned him into his presence to confront him with it. Armed with his impenetrable authority, he had summoned him. He had said: "See here, Dr. Pérez. Let me tell you what has just happened. A moment ago Marta, my daughter. . . ." And he recounted the scene to him summarily. Dr. Bartolomé Pérez had listened at first with a worried frown; then calmly, with even the hint of a smile. He commented: "Proof, sir, of a generous soul." That was his only remark. The bishop's myopic eyes had stared at him through his thick spectacles with stupefaction and then, instantly, with furious severity. But Dr. Pérez had not changed countenance; he had said—to top off the scandal—he had dared to ask: "And . . . does Your Excellency not intend to heed the voice of innocence?" The bishop—such was his shock—preferred not to answer at the moment. He was indignant, but, even more than indignant, he was thunderstruck. What could all that mean? How was so much obduracy possible? Or perhaps their influence extended to his very chambers—it would be too daring!—to the foot of his dais. Yet if they had dared to make use of his own daughter, why could they not have availed themselves as well of a priest, an Old Christian? He looked wonderingly, as though seeing him for the first time, at that blond peasant standing before him, undaunted, indifferent, firm as a rock (and, without being able to help it, he thought: "The brute!"), at that doctor and priest who was nothing but a boor, half-asleep in a routine of faith and, at the very bottom of all his knowledge, as unconscious as an ass. Next he tried to make himself feel compassion: such laxity, such complaisance in the midst of perils, was rather to be pitied. If it were up to people like that, he thought, religion was done for. They saw the danger growing everywhere, and they were not even aware of it. The bishop gave Dr. Pérez some instructions having nothing to do with the matter, and he dismissed him. Once again he was alone with his thoughts. By that time his anger had given way to lucid meditation. Something that, before now, he had been tempted to suspect on more than one occasion, now became very evident to him: that Old Christians, with all their proud carelessness, were bad guardians of Christ's citadel and risked damnation because of their excess of confidence. It was the eternal story, the parable whose meaning is ever renewed. No, sunk as they were in guilty confidence, they did not see—they could not see—the dangers, the subtle snares, the enemy's slinking maneuvers. They were brutish peasants, pagans almost, blockheads, with a poor idea of the Divinity, Mohammedans under Mohammed and Christians under Christ, according to the wind that flapped the banners; or else, those nobles engrossed in mortal disputes, or corrupted by their pact with the world, and no less oblivious to God. There was a reason why His Providence had led him—and would that others like him were in charge of every diocese—to the post of sentinel and captain of the Faith; for how can one who is off his guard resist a concealed, cunning attack, an ambush, a silent conspiracy within the fortress itself? As a warning, the good bishop would be reminded of an old family anecdote he had heard many times as a child to a chorus of his elders' unfailing guffaws: the adventure of his great-uncle, a wayward lad, a gadabout, who, in the Moorish kingdom of Almería, had embraced Islam without true conviction and, through his letters and arts, had managed to become the muezzin of a mosque in the midst of those barbarians. And whenever, from his lofty post, he saw one of those kinsfolk or acquaintances who denounced his defection crossing the square, he would raise his voice and, in the middle of the ritual Koranic invocation *La ilaha illa' llah,* interpolate among the Arabic words a string of insults in Hebrew against the false prophet Mohammed, giving the Jews to understand what, despite his unworthiness, was his true belief, to the derision of the pious, unsuspecting Moors, lost in their salaams. So too, in Castile, in all of Spain, many false converts now mocked unwary Christians, whose unbelievable confidence could only be explained by the lukewarm character of a religion handed down from fathers to sons, a religion in which they had always lived and triumphed, trusting, in the face of their enemies' affronts, to the ultimate justice of God. But oh! it was God, God Himself, who had made *him* the instrument of His justice on earth, for he knew the enemy camp and had the skill to expose its spies, and he would not allow himself to be deceived by tricks, like those used to deceive those lax believers who, in their weakness, even exchanged looks (yes, they had gone that far at times: he had caught them at it, understood them, exposed them), even went so far as to exchange looks of fear—a fear imbued, no doubt, with respect, admiration, and gratitude, but fear nonetheless—at the implacable rigor displayed by their prelate in defense of the Church. Had not Dr. Pérez himself spoken with a certain reticence on more than one occasion about the purging activities of his pastor? And yet, if the Messiah had come and had been made man and had founded the Church with the sacrifice of *His* divine blood, how could corruption be allowed to continue and grow in such a way, as if that sacrifice had been in vain?

For the time being, the bishop decided to dismiss Dr. Bartolomé Pérez from his service. It was not with teachers of that sort that one could give a tender child the strength necessary for a militant, besieged, and alert faith; and he did just what he had decided to do, without waiting until the next day. Even now, he felt uncomfortable, remembering the clear gaze that Dr. Pérez had directed at him on the occasion. Dr. Bartolomé Pérez had asked for no explanations, he had shown neither surprise nor anger. The dismissal scene had turned out to be incredibly easy—and for that reason all the more embarrassing! Between curious and, perhaps, ironic, the tutor had looked at His Excellency the bishop with his blue eyes, accepting without dispute the decision that separated him from tasks carried out for so many years and, seemingly, deprived him of the prelate's confidence. The same astonishing compliance with which he had received his dismissal confirmed the bishop in the justice of his decree, which he might have wished he could revoke, for Dr. Pérez's inability to defend himself, make allegations, argue, plead, and fight on his own behalf proved beyond a doubt that he lacked the fervor necessary to inspire steadfastness in another. And then, the very tears shed by the child when she learned of it bore witness to the gentle human affections in her soul, but not to the kind of solid religious training that implies a greater detachment from the everyday and transitory world.

This episode had been an invaluable warning to the bishop. He reorganized the operation of his household so that his daughter would enter adolescence, on whose threshold she

already stood, at her own pace. And he went ahead with the
indictment against his brother-in-law Lucero without allowing himself to be moved by any human consideration. Further
investigations uncovered other persons involved, the case was
extended to include them, and each new step showed how
widespread and deep-seated was the corruption whose stench
had first manifested itself in the person of Antonio María.
The action had come to take on enormous proportions; now,
piled there on his table, one could see all the dossiers; His
Excellency the bishop had the main documents set apart before him; he reviewed them, went over the most important
proceedings in his mind, and pondered again and again the
decisions he would have to face in court the next day. They
were weighty decisions. In the first place, the sentence against
those accused; but this sentence, despite its tremendous severity, was not the most painful part. The Judaizers' crime had
been established, clarified, and proven months ago, and in
the minds of all, accused and judges alike, this extreme sentence was taken for granted and needed only to be duly drawn
up and formalized. A more painful duty was to bring an indictment against Dr. Bartolomé Pérez, who, in consequence of
certain testimony, had been arrested the day before and confined in the prison of the Inquisition. One of those wretches,
in a last-minute, unpremeditated, extraneous declaration, had
attributed to Dr. Pérez some rather questionable opinions
which, at least, revealed the following alarming fact: that the
Old Christian and priest of Christ had had contacts, conversations, perhaps dealings with the group of Judaizers, and he had
done so not only after leaving the prelate's service, but before.
For his part, the prelate himself could not help but recall the
strange way in which, when he had informed him of little
Marta's intervention in behalf of her uncle Lucero, Dr. Pérez
had almost agreed with her, deviously supporting the child's

entreaty. Such an attitude, in the light of the evidence now emerging from these discoveries, took on a new meaning. And in view of all this, the good bishop could not, without violating his conscience, have abstained from initiating a thorough investigation, of the kind allowed only in the case of an indictment. God was his witness that he hated to decree it: the devilish substance of that whole business seemed to have a sort of gelatinous adhesiveness, it clung to one's hands, it spread out and threatened to soil everything; by now it even made him sick. He would gladly have disregarded it. But could he, in all conscience, ignore the signs that pointed so unequivocally to Dr. Bartolomé Pérez? In all conscience, he could not; even knowing, as he did, that this blow would recoil upon his own daughter. Since that day of disturbing memory—and three years had passed, during which the girl had grown into a woman—Marta had never again spoken to her father but with restraint and fear, resentful perhaps or, as he believed, overwhelmed by respect. She had swallowed her tears; she had asked no questions, she had sought—so far as he knew—no explanation. And, for that very reason, neither had the bishop dared, though he might have tried to hinder it, to forbid her from keeping Dr. Pérez as her confessor. He chose rather—he was sorry now for his weakness at that time—to adopt delaying tactics, since he had no valid arguments with which to oppose it openly. In short, the damage was done. What effect would it have on the unfortunate, innocent, generous creature when she learned, as she would without fail, that her confessor, her teacher, was being held prisoner on suspicions pertaining to matters of doctrine? All of which, on the other hand, might cast a shadow, discredit, upon her who had been his pupil, upon the bishop himself, who had named him tutor to his daughter. "The iniquity of the fathers . . ." he thought, wiping his brow.

A surge of compassionate tenderness flooded the dignitary's breast—tenderness toward the child who had grown up motherless, alone in the silent house, isolated from ordinary children, and under an all-too-imposing authority. He thrust his papers aside, put his pen into its holder, stood up, pushing back his armchair, went around the table and, with muffled steps, left his study, crossed, one after the other, two more rooms, almost groping his way, and, at last, gently opened partway the door of the bedroom where Marta was sleeping. Her slow, measured breathing could be heard within. Asleep, by the light of the oil lamp she seemed, not an adolescent, but a full-grown woman; her hand at her throat rose and fell with her breathing. All was still, in silence; and she slept there, in the shadows. The bishop looked at her for a long time; then, treading softly, he withdrew to his study and settled down again at his worktable to carry out, much to his regret, the dictates of his conscience. He worked all night. And when, near daybreak, he dosed off in spite of himself, his doubts, his inner struggle, the violence he had to inflict upon himself filled his sleep with disturbing shades. When Marta entered his study, as was her custom, early in the morning, the yellowish head with graying hair that rested heavily on his outstretched arms rose up suddenly; behind his spectacles, his myopic eyes opened wide in fright. And the girl, who had wanted to draw back, was nailed to the spot.

But the prelate also felt confused. He removed his spectacles and wiped the lenses with his sleeve, while half closing his eyes. Still very present, vivid in his memory, was what he had just dreamed: he had dreamed—precisely, about Marta—strange, disconcerting things that made him obscurely uneasy. In his dreams, he had seen himself high up in the minaret of a mosque, where he recited a litany, repeated, profuse, extravagant, chanted, and subtly burlesque, the meaning of which escaped even him. (What relation could there be—he thought—between this dream and the famous story of his kinsman, the false muezzin? Was he, too, perhaps a kind of false muezzin?) He shouted and shouted and kept on shouting the phrases of his absurd litany. But suddenly, from the foot of the tower, Marta's voice reached him, far, far away, faint but perfectly intelligible, saying to him—and the words, though distant, were very clear—"Your merits, father," it said, "have saved our people. You alone, my father, have redeemed all our line." At that moment the sleeping man had opened his eyes, and there stood Marta, across the table, looking at him with her clear gaze, while he, surprised, began to stir and sat up in his chair. He finished wiping his spectacles, regained his composure, arranged before him the dossiers spread across the table, and, running a hand over his brow, questioned his daughter. "Come here, Marta," he said in a neutral tone. "Come, tell me: if someone were to tell you that the merits of a virtuous Christian could revert to his ancestors and save them, what would you say?"

The girl looked at him, astonished. It was not unusual, in fact, for her father to put questions of doctrine to her: on that point the bishop had always watched over his daughter with the greatest care. But what sudden inspiration was this, now, upon awakening? She looked at him distrustfully; she thought for a moment; she answered, "Prayer and good works can, I believe, help the souls in purgatory, sir."

"Yes, yes," the bishop replied, "yes, but . . . what about the damned?"

She shook her head. "How can we know who is damned, father?"

The theologian had lent eyes and ears to her response. He was satisfied; he nodded. With a sign of his hand, he gave her permission to withdraw. She hesitated and, at last, she left the room.

But the bishop was not at ease. Alone now, and leafing through the folios, he still could not shake off a residue of distress. And, when once again he came upon Antonio María Lucero's declaration, extracted under torture, he suddenly remembered another of the dreams he had had a short while before, there, overcome by fatigue, his head leaning, perhaps, against the hard back of his chair. Stealthily, in the silence of the night—he dreamed—he had decided to go down to the dungeon where Lucero was awaiting justice, so as to convince him of his guilt and persuade him to be reconciled with the Church by begging forgiveness. Cautiously, then, he had started to open the door to the dungeon when—he dreamed—guards suddenly fell upon him and, without saying anything, without making a sound, began to carry him toward the rack. No one spoke a word; but without anyone's saying so, he knew that they had mistaken him for the prisoner Lucero and that they meant to put him through another interrogation. How turbid, how senseless dreams can be at times! He struggled, he fought, he tried to get free, but his efforts proved foolishly vain, like a child's, in the powerful arms of the guards. At first he thought that the annoying mistake would easily be set right simply by his speaking out. But when he tried to speak he noticed that they paid no attention—they did not even listen—and that high-handed treatment took away his self-confidence at once. Then he felt ridiculous, absolutely ridiculous, and—even stranger—guilty. Guilty of what? He did not know. But already he thought that he would inevitably be tortured. And he was almost resigned to it. What was most unbearable, however, was that Antonio María should see him like this, hanging by his feet like a chicken. For, suddenly, he was already suspended upside down, and Antonio María Lucero was looking at him; but he was looking at him as if he were a stranger; he was pretending to be disinterested, and, in the meanwhile, nobody was listening to his protests. But *he*

was—he, the real culprit, lost and hidden among the indis-
tinguishable officials of the Holy Tribunal, was perfectly
aware of the mistake. But he was feigning ignorance; he was
looking on with hypocritical indifference. Neither threats nor
promises nor entreaties could shake his hypocritical indifference. There was no one to come to his rescue. And only
Marta, who, inexplicably, had also appeared there, would
every now and then wipe, with cunning skill, the sweat from
his face.

His Excellency the bishop passed a handkerchief across his
brow. He rang a small copper bell that was on the table and
asked for a glass of water. He waited a moment for it, and
when it came he drank it in one long, anxious swallow and, at
once, began again to work eagerly on his papers—now lit,
thank God, by a ray of fresh sunlight—until, a little later, the
secretary of the Holy Office arrived.

His Excellency was still dictating the final text of the contemplated resolutions—and noon was drawing near—when,
to the surprise of both officials, the door flew open and they
saw Marta rush wildly into the room. She entered like a whirl-
wind, but in the middle of the room she came to a halt and,
fixing her shining eyes on her father, disregarding the presence of his subordinate and without any preamble, she all but
shouted at him, point-blank, "What has happened to Dr.
Pérez?" And she waited in strained silence.

The bishop's eyes blinked behind his spectacles. He said
nothing for a moment; he did not react as might have been
expected, as he would have expected of himself. And the
secretary could not believe his ears nor get over his astonishment when he at last heard him venture a faltering reply:
"What is all this, child? Calm yourself. What's the matter?
Dr. Pérez is going to be . . . he's going to make a declaration.
We all hope there is no cause . . . but," he recovered, at-

tempting a tone of benevolent severity, "what is the meaning of this, Marta?"

"They've arrested him. He's under arrest. Why is he under arrest?" she persisted, very excited, her voice trembling. "I must know what's going on."

The bishop hesitated for an instant in the face of her extraordinary outburst. Then, after directing a weak smile of understanding to the secretary, as though asking for his sympathy, he began to sketch a confused explanation about how it was necessary to fulfill certain formalities that, no doubt, sometimes caused unjustified hardships, but which were required in view of the higher aim of maintaining a close watch in defense of the Faith and doctrine of Our Lord Jesus Christ, et cetera. A long, jumbled, and sometimes disconnected speech from which it was easy to see that his words were following a different path than his thoughts. While it went on, Marta's flashing gaze plunged onto the tiled floor of the room, was caught up in the moldings of the dais, and, finally, rose again, vibrant as a sword, when the girl, in a tone belying the studied, doubtful moderation of her words, interrupted the prelate.

"I dare not think," she said, "that if my father had been in Caiaphas' place, he too would not have recognized the Messiah."

"What do you mean by that?" the bishop shrieked in alarm.

" 'Judge not, that ye be not judged.' "

"What do you mean by that?" he repeated in confusion.

"Judge, judge, judge." Now Marta's voice was angry; and yet very sad, dejected, almost inaudible.

"What do you mean by that?" he threatened, enraged.

"I wonder," she responded slowly, her eyes on the floor, "how one can be sure that the Second Coming will not happen as secretly as the first."

This time it was the secretary who spoke. "The Second Coming?" he murmured, as though to himself; and he began to shake his head. The bishop, who had turned pale on hearing his daughter's words, gave the secretary a troubled, anguished look. The secretary kept on shaking his head.

"Be silent!" the prelate ordered from his chair of state.

And she, emboldened, violent: "How do we know," she shouted, "that among those whom you daily imprison, and torture, and condemn, is not to be found the Son of God?"

"The Son of God!" the secretary marveled. He seemed scandalized; he looked expectantly at the bishop.

And the bishop, terrified: "My daughter, do you know what you are saying?"

"Yes, I know. I know very well. You may, if you wish, have me arrested."

"You've gone mad. Go away."

"Do you mean that you won't indict me because I'm your daughter? You would have the Messiah Himself burned at the stake!"

His Excellency the bishop bent his brow, beaded with sweat; his lips trembled in supplication: "Help me, Father Abraham!" and he made a sign to the secretary. The secretary understood; he expected nothing less. He drew out a clean sheet of paper, dipped his pen in the inkwell, and for some time all that was heard was its scratching on the rough paper, while the prelate, pale as a corpse, stared at his fingernails.

The Embrace

"**L**and of salt and iron. Violent, thirsty, rugged land. Ocher land. Flower of rosemary, yellow hedge mustard, pine groves of perennial and bitter green. Horses, bulls, goats, dirty sheep, shepherds with hard eyes. Brambles, hawthorn, great rocks, blood, clay, dust. My land, farewell!" It was Don Juan Alfonso's[*] eyes that were taking leave; his lips trembled in silence. He had brought his horse to a halt by the river so as to catch his breath. Beneath the cliff, the current roared in the gorge, like the horseman's heart in his throat. He had galloped from midnight till dawn, his white beard streaming over his shoulder. No sooner had he noticed that his master was sinking down, scarcely had he seen Don Pedro's[†] hand open on the ground and let go of the glittering knife than he had slipped away and, leaving the castle, jumped on a horse, crossed the camp, and fled, cutting across the lands of Toledo. He had seen the king fall, and he was escaping from the Bastard's men before the news could get ahead of him and reach the borders of the realm. He dreaded the fear of all the irresolute people who would now try and

[*]Don Juan Alfonso de Alburquerque, favorite of King Pedro I.
[†]Pedro I the Cruel (1334–69), sometimes called the Justiciar, king of Castile and León (see p. 49n). His reign, chronicled by Pedro López de Ayala, was marked by constant civil war with his illegitimate half-brothers.

make up for their past vacillations with some hasty evidence
of zeal. And what better, more pleasing tribute to the new
king, he thought, than to deliver up to him, hands bound
behind his back, the venerable man who over twenty years of
war had been counselor and sagacious mentor to his recently
defeated brother?

Once more, the old man's eyes swept across the indifferent
land, and then he forded the river and rode at a slow gait into
an oak grove, seeking rest for his weary bones. Leaning against
a tree, at last he wept for Don Pedro's death. The fratricidal
embrace, which had held the retinues of both kings breathless
in the castle hall, was for him the harbinger of his own agony.
And now, weeping for his master, he wept for himself.

Twenty years of constant struggle! Twenty years, and he
remembered the beginnings of that disastrous reign even
more clearly than its turbid end, which had come about the
night before. Twenty years! The mighty king Don Alfonso *
had fallen at the peak of his power. He was besieging the
fortress of Gibraltar when the plague overcame his body's
defenses, treacherously felling that giant of the invincible
arm. And he, Don Juan Alfonso, tutor to the Prince Royal,
and field marshal during the final days of the king's fever,
had made provision for and ordered the transfer to Seville
of his mortal remains. Uneasiness had hovered around his
soul with the dark tenacity of a horsefly during the bustle of
the first preparations and along the sad stages of the
journey, when the cortege took the road to the Court,
across Andalusia, through olive groves, accompanied always, night and day, by the strident chirp of the cicada.
From the camp at Gibraltar to Seville, Don Juan Alfonso
had time to brood over his fears and to instruct his royal

---

*Alfonso XI (1312–50), a strong and capable king of Castile, died
prematurely of the plague while besieging Gibraltar.

ward about the dangers he felt weighing on his heart. Behind the coffin, graced with the standard and followed by the dead king's charger, he rode beside the new king, Don Pedro, and gave him his counsel.

"My lord and son," he said, "the trials of war your tender years have known till now are nothing compared to those that await you in your reign. A grown king must betray weakness before anyone dares disobey him, but a young king must prove his strength so that no one dares. All the more so if those in a position to disobey are powerful and of his own blood."

"Do you speak of the bastards, Juan Alfonso?" Don Pedro had replied. "I will make them feel I'm the king."

"It would be better for you to make them feel that you're their brother," his tutor observed gravely. "And I want you to know what your father's words were when he charged me——"

"But am I not the king?"

"You are. But by the violence of your blood you must measure theirs."

"I will master it, I promise."

"You are strong enough, my son, I know. But perhaps your prudence is still young. You must learn prudence from that great lord we are taking home to bury."

"Was it prudence on his part to fill the realm with bastards, nourished and raised in envy toward a younger brother, whom they hated already in his mother's womb?"

"Ah, Don Pedro, from the breasts of your mother you yourself sucked hatred for the sons of Doña Leonor.* Unlucky Don Pedro, your passion keeps you from choosing your words and knowing when to say them."

---

*Doña Leonor de Guzmán (ca. 1310–51) was the mistress of Alfonso XI and the mother of a number of bastard sons including Enrique de Trastamara, the firstborn; his twin brother, Fadrique, grand master of Alcántara; and Tello.

"But tell me, why do you speak of prudence? Was that prudence? Tell me, for God's sake. . . ."

They rode on a space with their heads bent, more from the weight of their thoughts than from the force of the sun, which was now well up in the sky. After a while, the tutor spoke again:

"Perhaps it is bold of me to admonish one already my king. But I do so, Pedro, my son, out of obedience to him who is now dead, and my mouth will echo words of your father's, now silenced. I beg you to hear them as his words, for I shall repeat to you what our good king Don Alfonso said to me before giving up his soul to the King of Heaven. So listen to me with respect, and God grant that your father's admonitions be graven in your heart as they are in my memory."

He paused. And—since the young man was silent—he went on:

"You must know that, seeing his death draw near, our lord Don Alfonso called me to his side and charged me with the guidance of your youth. It was hard to hold back my tears when I saw how little the good king cared about losing his life for the sake of life itself, and how much because he was abandoning you amid so many perils and pitfalls. But you must understand: by pitfalls he meant those of youthful imprudence rather than those coming from the hostility of others. If that accursed plague had not cut short his life in its prime, and had allowed it to reach its natural end, the Crown would have fallen to you at a time when your feats of arms and ability to govern would have already forged your fame and tempered your judgment. What could you have feared then from those great lords? The sons of Doña Leonor de Guzmán, enriched and honored by their father, the king Don Alfonso, would then have been the best and strongest vassals of their brother the king Don Pedro, and their mothers' mutual hatred would have been dampened by old age or perhaps extinguished by death. But, since God decreed otherwise, your father charged me to stay at your side and to help you with my counsel, the fruit of my years and of the experience acquired at his side."

"And what, through your mouth, does my father the king Don Alfonso command me to do?"

"He advises you, King Don Pedro, above all, that Doña Leonor de Guzmán not be disturbed, either in her person or in her property. Everything that he gave her must be honored as hers. And if you think about it, this is the advice of a fine statesman, and not just that of a fine gentleman. For time, dissipating the fears that lady must now feel, will also disarm her precautions. Or, at least, you will have been able to avoid her assuming an attitude of defiance toward the Court, and using it to instigate a revolt in which she would not lack for help—beginning, one would expect, with that of her own sons."

"He who begat them must have known them well. And, knowing them, he died fearing their treachery. What else? Go on, good counselor."

"As for your brothers, the king (may he rest in peace) said to me: 'They are all magnanimous, and all proud. What may lead them someday to join with Don Pedro is not love, but honor. Try, Juan Alfonso, my old friend, my companion (and as he said these words he pressed my hand imploringly), try to guide the realm toward great enterprises, like this war we are waging against the infidels, and let my son ask the help of his brothers—for to ask in God's cause is no dishonor. Doing battle together, sharing triumphs and dangers, their hearts will join in brotherhood." And he said more. He said that since you are above them in station and inferior in age, it would be fitting for you to reach out to them with a friendly gesture. That in the necessarily confused and distrustful early days of a reign, such a gesture can be the best augury. That you should bear in mind, above all, the gentle nature of Don Fadrique and make of his friendship a bridge toward the goodwill of your other brothers, who are more hardhearted and proud: Don Enrique, always tempted by ambition; Don Tello, always on the verge of losing his temper. For Don Fadrique does not curb with cunning an impatient heart, nor does he easily give way to anger. He likes music, he makes merry with his friends, and he's always open to a good word."

"Good and wise are the words of my father the king, and I shall abide by his counsel, which is also yours, my lord Don Juan Alfonso," Don Pedro answered after a time.

"May God grant that it be so," his tutor exclaimed.

Before the funeral train had traveled half the distance, news of the king's death had already reached the Alcazar of Seville, where Queen María was residing. And so, while the old tutor was advising the Prince Royal behind Don Alfonso's coffin, the ill-advised widow was ordering that her enemy, Doña Leonor de Guzmán, be beheaded. Arranging for the concubine's punishment before her husband's funeral, the queen summoned a group of her followers and gave them hasty, furious instructions to go at once to Medina Sidonia, where Doña Leonor was living, and to bring her back her rival's head. From her window, she sent them off with shouts of dreadful urgency: "Hurry, hurry! Run! I've grown old waiting, and I can't wait another day. That accursed woman took my life from me inch by inch. Take hers with a single stroke. I want to hold her head in my hands before Sunday."

Her final cries rang out like a howl. When the horsemen had passed beyond the gate, the queen went into her chamber with dry and shining eyes. All the bells of Seville were tolling, but Doña María could not think about the dead king. Her only thoughts were for the concubine who had given him so many sons, and whose fortune and power had grown with her sons, while she, the wretched queen, raised her Don Pedro and kept the house of her ever-absent lord. "Why should I mourn his death," she thought, "if he wasn't mine when he was alive? *I* lived only for *him;* he, for the other woman. She robbed me of my life. No, she cannot pay for it with this single, sudden stroke." And Doña María looked back upon the years of that life of longing, always on the lookout, always asking questions, always putting two and two together, always clinging to Don Alfonso who, for his part, appeared more and more formal, deferential, and reserved toward her. In all his manners, gestures, and words she thought she found traces of the other woman, whom she never saw but about whom she was always receiving reports that would make her turn pale and weep. Twenty-eight years had passed since the one occasion on which she met Doña Leonor, and she still could not forget her smile, at once forced and happy. She remembered the color of her headdress, her finery, the brocade of her cloak, the black ribbon at her throat, her lofty stature that showed her to even more advantage as she curtsied to the slight figure of the queen. And now, while waiting for her terrible order to be carried out, she was reminded, again and again, each time in clearer detail, of that far-off scene that fanned her hatred. She could not sleep until her emissaries, on their return, handed her the bloody token.

Doña María dismissed everyone and remained alone with the dreadful bundle on her lap. Its weight seemed to make her legs grow weak. After a while she untied the ends of the kerchief and, standing up, raised as high as her own head the bloodless head of Doña Leonor: its mouth distorted, its gray locks matted together with clots of blood. The queen—with that strangely small, worn, blurred head between her hands— burst out crying from fatigue. But at that very moment the bells began to toll, announcing the arrival of the cortege bearing the dead king. She composed herself; she set the head on the table, splashed cold water on her face, and rang a little silver bell to give her orders.

Through one gate the body of the dead king entered Seville, and through the other arrived word that his sons, the bastards, were fortifying themselves in their castles. When—in the cathedral, during the service—Don Juan Alfonso learned the fearful news, he felt the premonition that had been hovering over his head all along the way suddenly swoop down upon his heavy heart. Amid the clouds of incense and the grave tones of the ritual chant, he saw the disastrous end of that reign rising inexorably before him.

And yet that destiny would advance slowly through the years, wearily, heavily, in tortuous episodes—tortuous and senselessly cruel—in which not only the furies of the blood were to play their part, but also, in a mysterious way, even endeavors of goodwill. Of what use against such a destiny were the calculations of prudence, wise measures, or a statesman's skill? Of what use, indeed, was the effort undertaken and carried on for many months by Don Juan Alfonso's goodwill to try and dispell the horror instilled in the House of Guzmán by the foolish queen with her revenge? Of what use the long-drawn-out negotiations, the protestations, the promises and gifts? Of what use the endeavors of the good men of the realm? Vile incidents always poisoned the fruit of the best intentions. And that is how, not long thereafter, the grand master* Don Fadrique set out toward death along the very path that should have led him to the favor of the king. For the latter, persuaded at last, full of benevolence, had summoned him to his presence so as to settle face to face, amicably, the vexing contest

*See p. 47n.

for the grand mastership. He was awaiting him in the Alcazar, prepared to press to his heart the brother he had never seen and whose gentleness he had so often heard praised, when someone brought him, at the last minute, a denunciation of his duplicity. He learned for certain that, before responding to his summons, the grand master of Alcántara had met to take counsel with the other bastards and, full of irreconcilable rancor, had complained before them of the king who was curtailing his privileges. They were even able to repeat the exact nature of his bitter words: "What sort of grand master am I?" they reported he had said. "One by one, he has stripped me of all my prerogatives. I am no longer even allowed to enter the castles of the Order without his consent. The cross on my habit has become a brand of ignominy upon my breast." And so he had recapitulated his bitter quarrel in tireless detail. At last, tears of rage and shame had streamed from his eyes when he recalled the insolent scene in which a garrison of soldiers, out of obedience to the king, had refused entrance to the grand master, their liege lord. "Exhortations, threats—all useless! I was obliged to turn back, humiliated. How do I know," he concluded, "why I'm now summoned to the Alcazar? Should I go?" It seems the brothers had agreed, after much discussion, that Don Fadrique should repair to Seville pretending to be moved by a conciliatory spirit and, after securing from Don Pedro whatever concessions he could, use them perhaps at a later date against his tyranny. That was the secret information they brought him: the news had sped toward the king's chamber faster than the grand master himself. And when they announced his arrival and he had him there, in person, before the gates, the disposition of the king's will had changed, and anger burned in his breast, fed by revulsion at his former good intentions. So the deceiver was there, was he?

Don Pedro leaned out the window and saw below the grand master's company, all riding white horses with scarlet trappings. The men of his escort had stayed behind in the courtyard to wait, while Don Fadrique dismounted and entered the palace alone. He had not yet climbed the first flight of stairs when he heard—and the smile froze on his lips—the loud voice that, from over the balustrade, hurled a death order at him. "Macebearers," it cried, "death to the grand master of Alcántara!" Don Fadrique raised his head and for the first time his eyes, terrified, met the angry eyes of his brother Pedro. "Treason!" exclaimed the grand master, his voice hoarse with fright. And the king's enraged, trembling voice pursued him down the stairs: "Yes, bastard! Yes! Treason for treason!" Soldiers with maces appeared from everywhere to intercept the fugitive's path. Some were already waiting for him at the foot of the staircase, while others ran down behind him, threatening his head with the iron heads of their maces. The grand master jumped, his unsheathed dagger in his right hand, and somehow made his way among the groups besieging him, fleeing through corridors and galleries. Closely pursued, he took refuge in a chamber. A thread of blood, trickling from his lacerated brow, stained his curly blond beard. Cornered, he shielded his head with his left arm, and, brandishing the blade of his fine dagger in his right hand, he managed to escape from them again, running toward the main hall. But his strength was gone: he stopped, and collapsed. Once on the ground, a final blow split his skull.

All this had happened swiftly and in silence, entirely unknown to the escort waiting outside. "Every man to his post!" the king ordered. Then he approached the grand master's body and bent over it to stare in amazement: on its mangled temple he saw, matted with blood and sweat, blond locks very like those that curled over his own ears; and the bloodied, contracted mouth also made the same fleshy line that, on Don Pedro's face, was a copy of the dead King Alfonso's. But, in contrast, the grand master's small, delicate, smooth hand, with its sparkling ring and toylike dagger, bore no resemblance to the broad, stubby, strong hands of Don Pedro. Looking away from the shattered head, the king fixed his eyes on that strange, feminine hand, the sign of his treachery. "The grand master Don Fadrique is best dead," he muttered as he withdrew.

With that, the bridges were burned: henceforth the brothers would always be enemies. Had he only been able to curb his anger, to dissemble it. . . . But it was now beyond help: as a fire that having crept lazily across the ground for some time may rise up to the heavens with sudden impetus, so at that time violence spread in Castile, destroying everything in sight. Resting his head against the trunk of the oak tree on which he was leaning, Don Juan Alfonso gazed wearily out over the lands he was about to forsake. His eyelids heavy, his eyes smarting, the fiery passions that had devastated the realm for years and years appeared to him in the familiar vision of blazing fields: crops ruined, the sweat of an entire village burned with the cars of grain, smoke, black wounds of the stubble, charred stone of the threshing floors. My poor Don Pedro, now fallen forever! The old tutor had seen from the start that end which, nonetheless, he had fought so hard to prevent. So many warnings, so many caveats, so many sleepless nights, so many sorrows! You labor, you sweat, you endure hardships—all in vain! In vain Don Juan Alfonso had struggled to carry out the charge his master the king had given him on his deathbed. With all the weight of his statecraft, of his letters and his goodwill, he had been able to do as little as the dead man in his tomb, whose sons were ripping up the country and leaving it in bloody tatters. He had been able to do as little during the life of his ward Don Pedro as he could now that Don Pedro had fallen beneath Don Enrique's dagger and he himself, a fugitive from death, an exile, was calling up the inconsistent shadows of what had been.

"Who can curb runaway horses," the old man thought, "and what force do words of reason command? You work out your move, you carefully position your bishop and castle. You've devised a plan, and you delight in fancying how your opponent will struggle and succumb to the subtle mastery of your game. But an impatient sweep of his hand defeats all your combinations, or else knocks over the chessboard in a downfall of kings and queens. Then what? Why, start all over again!" Don Juan Alfonso recalled features, isolated profiles of a vague and distant scene in which, when he was playing chess with the young king, Don Pedro had destroyed the game on the point of losing. He could see his broad and freckled hand fall awkwardly on the two armies joined in battle and sweep them both away, the red and white pieces mixed together. And he could see more: he saw the king's knees push over the light table, his body rise and, once on its feet, begin to walk up and down the hall, pacing angrily, irately, before their silent expectation. Who was the other man, standing near the chess table, who followed the young man's furious movements with him? It was Don Samuel Leví!* Now, all at once, the whole scene came back to him: Don Samuel, the treasurer, had with catlike steps come up to Don Pedro and stopped to follow the progress of the game in silence, only sighing from time to time, until, taking advantage of a pause, he caught the king's attention with a single phrase. He was reporting the assault made on the Jewry of Toledo by Don

*Treasurer of Castile, counselor and friend of Pedro I.

Enrique's men, just as he had heard it a moment before from the lips of his nephew, José Leví, a child of fifteen, who had come to him after escaping from the disaster. Don Samuel began his story impersonally; but soon, his hands clasped together, he was describing what the boy had told him, as though he himself had seen it with his own eyes. The family had just finished the midday meal and they were still at table, eating sweets and talking quietly, when suddenly the door flew open and one of the maidservants appeared in it, terrified, with her hands above her head: "They're coming, they're here!" Before she could explain the cause of her fear, the mob rushed in and destroyed everything in an instant. From inside the wardrobe where he had hidden, the boy beheld the cruel scene. Paralyzed with terror, José saw the hatchet that split his father's venerable head, and the hairy hands that grasped its handle were the hands of another José, José Rodríguez, the journeyman harness maker who had for two years, without success, sought the hand of his sister Estrella. Now he had her prostrate at his feet, whiter and paler than her name, * and he was about to rape her unconscious body while other villains plundered the house, filling sacks and kerchiefs with clinking silver. All this the young man had to witness from his hiding place. The vicious horde panted as it toiled, sending forth shouts of greed and, at times, lapsing into incredible silence. How could they not yet have discovered him, there in his hiding place? He could bear it no longer. He came out of the wardrobe, went to kneel down before the harness maker, and bowed his head, expecting death. But, instead of granting it, that coarse hand passed through his tangled mop of hair with unlikely gentleness, almost with affection. The rear of the house had already begun to burn. The crowd fled, and the

*Estrella: star.

poor boy ran away too. No one paid any attention to him; no one. At nightfall, he lay down to sleep beneath the bridge over the Tagus, and with the break of day he set off toward Seville, in search of his powerful uncle.

Hearing this story, told in a monotone whine, Don Pedro had gone wild with rage. He overturned the chess board, while his treasurer and his tutor looked at one another in dismay. Where would that rage lead to? The king's outbursts were utterly unpredictable. He was as likely to shrug, to remain indifferent, as he was to order punishments that left the world aghast. With ice in his veins, Don Juan Alfonso remembered his exemplary punishment of the archdeacon whom he ordered buried alive next to the corpse of the poor shoemaker left unburied by clerical greed. What consideration would stop that madman? Had he not once even raised his hand against his own mother so as to defend the name of his mistress Doña María de Padilla?* A long time had passed; the object of many of the efforts in which he had spent his life had vanished, and the old quarrels had been irrevocably resolved and decided. But the memory of that shameful palace argument in which Don Pedro had threatened the queen brought back in a moment the whole train of his revulsion, indignation, dismay, and worry. Once more the old tutor felt the terror that had paralyzed him then, when the young man's insane daring had shown him once again that everything could only end badly. Badly for everyone. First of all, for himself, for the vigilant and faithful Juan Alfonso who, with no firm support, with no strength of his own on which to base his position, had to try to inspire the conduct of so proud a ward with prudence. For even Don Samuel Leví was more powerful than he: he had the gold; that was his strength. But

*The mistress of Pedro I, who was brought up in the house of her uncle, Don Juan Alfonso de Alburquerque. She died in 1361.

he himself could count on nothing but the king's goodwill, and his only rein on his capricious shifts of fancy was Don Pedro's love for Doña María de Padilla, that niece of his, to whom, after she was orphaned, Juan Alfonso had been a second father. On this lady alone his favor with the king depended. How could he not help trembling when he saw the brute was rashly playing her off against the old queen, which could only set the whole Court against her! Wasn't the hostility of his brothers, the powerful bastards, masters of half of Castile, enough for the king? Did he have to stir up dissension within his own household?

No, his wise judgment, the tact and moderation of his opinions were useless against so much folly heaped on folly. For if the way in which the king always defended his María de Padilla against everyone had been outrageous and imprudent, no less absurd was the attempt of the queen and her relatives to apply to his supposed malady the remedy of his marriage to the princess from France. He, Don Juan Alfonso, had opposed the unfortunate scheme with all his might and with recourses of all sorts, including—why not?—those of intrigue. "A hidden interest!" they immediately shouted at him. How many calumnies had poured down upon his head then! Why a hidden interest? What harm could a political alliance—and at bottom that match was nothing more—have done to the long-established liaison of the king with his mistress? And, in the end, what did all that matter to *him*? Just because Don Pedro's concubine was his niece, people supposed that life was easy for him. Yes, they call that easy! Except that he knew that headstrong colt well. And, because he knew him well, he had tried, though without success, to oppose the marriage. Time was not long in proving him right. Doña Blanca* arrived from France: her eyes

*Doña Blanca de Borbón, or Blanche de Bourbon (1335–61), daughter of Pierre I, duc de Bourbon, and Isabeau de Valois, married Pedro I in 1353.

proud, her lips compressed—a mere child! God knows he felt
sorry for her when he saw her. And what character, in one so
young; what a way of never uttering a word, not a single one,
ever! Lord, how pride can sustain one in misfortune! The outcome was that the old queen, having abused him so for opposing the marriage (yes, the old harpy was the one who had driven
her claws deepest into his reputation, who had loaded him with
the vilest insults), had then been forced to cast about for ways
to alleviate the very damage he had tried to avert, ways with
which she hoped to amend the consequences of her son's gross
conduct. And, like her, all those who had done what they
could to bring about the match were now rushing to prevent
what threatened to be, as indeed it became, the only fruit of
that marriage: a monster of new discord. Above all, they tried
to constrain Don Pedro's conduct by adding coercion to their
pleas that he mend his ways.

Forgetting for a moment the precarious situation in which
he found himself—fleeing into exile and in danger of his
life—the old man Don Juan Alfonso was tempted to laugh
when he remembered the wealth of precautions taken in con-
nection with that memorable palace plot, and how Don Pedro's natural vigor, that time masked by cunning, smashed
their carefully worked-out plans in a single blow and frustrated
the officious efforts of his relatives, determined as they were to
make him see reason. There indeed the Queen Mother's stubborn rancor had made the right prognosis. "It will all be
useless," she had assured her lady-in-waiting, who was dress-
ing her to attend the family council convened in the city of
Toro. "Useless, Juana! I've come to this meeting, not because
I have any confidence in its results, but because, being who I
am, I could not stay away. But I know very well how useless it
is. My relations think the malady can be remedied. It would
be a great deal if it were merely alleviated. I don't expect that.

As if I didn't know the roots of that malady! Very bitter roots. They may get him to go back to his wife, they can lock him up with her in her chamber if they like, tie him to the bedstead. His mind will be with the other woman, his face will smile like an idiot's, while you feel yourself dying a thousand times at his side! No, no." And she shook her head.

"Perhaps, my lady, they've given him a philter of some sort," her lady-in-waiting ventured, just to say something, as she kneeled beside her pinning her camisole.

"A philter? Yes, that could be. Any kind of evil is possible. But since my Don Pedro is so young, what better philter than the wiles of an artful woman?"

"Certainly, my lady. And as she's so beautiful——"

"What are you saying, you fool? Her beauty is as false as her soul! You see, Juana? You too are deceived by her reputation! Beautiful, they say. Yet I ask myself, 'Where does her beauty lie?' Had you known her, as I did, when she was a little girl running around the Alcazar gardens while her uncle Juan Alfonso, already so foresighted, was dispatching business inside, you wouldn't be praising that false beauty now. I can assure you, she had the face of a little devil. And how has she changed from that time to this? Is her complexion any more fair? Have her shiny little eyes by chance grown large and clear? That enormous mouth of hers, always laughing, has it perhaps become small and modest? Anyone would be blind not to see where that so-called beauty comes from. Anyone would be a hypocrite to praise it. For what they praise in her as beauty has another, more suitable, name."

"It's very true, my lady, that Doña María's features are far from perfect, and of course they can't have changed. But anyone who's known her, not as a little girl, but since her coming of age, can recognize in the whole something that disguises——"

"Exactly! You said it—disguises. She's the devil in disguise, concealed beneath rich Murcian* fabrics. But, how can the image of lust be called beautiful, however much it may be disguised beneath false modesty? That's something I'll never understand. Those bitches are all alike! What is it they have? What do they give to men? A philter, that's right. A philter!"

The queen fell silent. To break that silence, her lady-in-waiting observed contritely, "But, my lady, the king is still so young . . ."

"Hush, woman! Be quiet, for God's sake!" she snapped back. "Don't I know what that devilish bent is like? I know the old tune by heart: 'He's so young! He'll improve with time. . . .' Let those who don't know where the king got his disposition fool themselves if they choose. *I* am not fooled. I can't be fooled. And now you see what's happened: they thought everything would be set right by bringing him that princess from France, and it's only made him wallow deeper in vice. They didn't count on his natural aversion to all that is noble and worthy. Poor princess, poor innocent child, poor Doña Blanca! You see what he's like. He flees from her chamber the very night of the wedding and, mad with desire, riding roughshod over all the proprieties, goes to the bedroom of his concubine. What could she offer him, spoiled as he is by the Moorish luxury, the pearls, the Oriental perfumes he so liberally gives her for his own pleasure? Everything set right, indeed. I suppose they think his malady can be cured. Well, Juana, I must attend this assembly because they've asked me to, and there's no way out of it. But I mean to take no part in it—I won't even open my mouth. Amen to everything! They'll soon see how little this gathering of good intentions can accomplish."

*Murcia, in southeastern Spain, spent many centuries under Moslem rule. It had an important silk industry.

True to her word, the Queen Mother had in fact kept silent all during the meeting. When, having been lured there by deceit, Don Pedro appeared in the great hall of Toro Castle before his noble kinsmen, it was his aunt, the aged queen of Aragon—the one responsible for that extraordinary family council—who also took upon herself the weighty task of admonishing him. She reproached him for preferring the company of knaves, she tried to make him see the risks and dangers of turning away from the powerful, and she ended by saying, with words that history would record, "It better suits your dignity to be accompanied, as you now are, by all the good and noble men of your realm." Then, softening the severity of her tone, she went on:

"It's true that a good king should protect all men. But, my lord and nephew, you must know that your liking for the common people offends those of us who are your equals. In whom do you place your friendship, your trust? It shames one to say: in Jews, in merchants, in converts. To whom do you give the offices of your royal household? To people who were nobodies yesterday, and who are unbelievably arrogant today. People whose mere presence is annoying, not to mention their conceit. And to whom do you tell all your plans? Whom do you consult about your every action? For God's sake, nephew, it's almost more than one can bear. Not even to answer this summons of ours could you dispense with that Don Leví of yours, who gets rich on what he collects for you and governs the realm with his coffers."

She paused and, gripping the arms of her chair, leaned forward to sum up in a trembling voice: "So as to prevent greater evils from befalling you, and the reputation of your powerful enemies from increasing at the expense of your own, those of us who care for you have decided to serve you personally in the offices of your household and your realm. Under-

stand, my lord, that we do this out of love for you, and
without derogation of your authority—now stained by the
base persons with whom you surround yourself."

All those present sought the king's eyes, but in vain. Don
Pedro had listened, his head down and his face dark—that expression, so peculiar to him, of anger that grows and grows in
silence until it erupts in a fit of rage. The presence of the princes
and the grandees, in league against him and lending quiet support to the words of the queen of Aragon, was as embarrassing
to him as it was irritating. When, with his aunt's final words, he
had become aware of the situation, he glanced quickly at his
mother, who lowered her eyes and immediately resumed her
sullen air. Now, at last, he realized where all this was leading.
With no change in his expression, he heard them arrest his
treasurer and all his attendants in the antechambers, and he
watched his kinsmen distribute the royal posts among themselves. But when he thought his chance had come, he rose from
his seat, made his way out with studied sobriety, went down to
the courtyard without anyone's daring to stop him, and,
mounting his horse, galloped off alone into the countryside.

Don Juan Alfonso, who himself had also had to flee on
horseback, though with no other hope than to save his
wretched and weary life, laughed now when he recalled the
effortless dispatch with which his master had then turned the
tables on the grandees of the realm. And that laugh, spontaneous and uncontainable, roused him for a moment from his
despondent state.

Yes, Don Pedro had restored his authority with swift and
easy resolution. And once the most urgent decisions had been
made, he repaired to his mistress to unload the burden of his
sorrow in her lap. How lovingly she must have listened to his
voice in the darkness! Without the support of his strong
mouth, without the backing of his wild eyes, without the

corroboration of his savage hand, his was no longer a full voice that inspired fear, but a voice that trembled in a sort of helplessness upon descending from its habitual resonance into melancholy tones. Turbid and embittered, it complained:

"Everything, everything is united against me. Everything beats me down. Even my own mother turns on me and burdens me with reproaches. As if she were not guilty. . . . What is the source of all my misfortunes, if not the revenge she took on old Doña Leonor? At that time she could not curb her bitterness, and now, when I must fight to stem the flood that she herself unloosed, she dares to belittle me. Only in your arms can I find peace, María."

"Poor darling! Poor, sweet silver brow, sweet golden curls! Why must you bear the weight of that crown?" she answered. "My Pedro, what wouldn't I give to free you of that weight, so that you would be mine alone!"

"No, not that. Never. Do you think that the crown weighs me down? I was born a king! No, what weighs me down and fills me with bitterness, and stirs me up until I'm sick, is the misery of having to fight my own kind. They all want to rule me. They all want to take my freedom from me, as if instead of being king I were the lowliest slave. I prefer having to do with declared enemies. My brothers have declared themselves my enemies, and they'll meet me as an enemy. One by one they'll fall with their throats slit—I swear it! But why does my own mother want to bind my hands, she whose hands were once so hasty? Why does Juan Alfonso, your kinsman, want to control my will by pretending to submit to it? Why does even the ghost of my father (may God forgive him!) also want to take away my strength and make the task he bequeathed me even harder with so many powerful, rebellious bastards?"

"You know my uncle Juan Alfonso is the only faithful supporter we have at Court, Pedro dear."

"You defend him, and rightly so. As he defends you against the hatred of all. Well done! But tell me, why must I be the only one with no kinsmen to lean upon? The word brother means enemy to me. And I can't even trust that of mother."

"She seeks what she believes is best for you as king. She desires greatness for her son. And then, you must remember that a woman who is queen, and who has spent her life oppressed by the demands of royal decorum, cannot begin to understand what is between us, and she must abhor it. Out of love for her son, she abhors me. What weighs upon my heart is knowing that, at bottom, I am the cause of your troubles. Yes, don't say I'm not. I know. Didn't all this begin with your marriage to Doña Blanca? Well, that marriage was arranged not so much to help the realm as out of hatred for me, a hatred, I tell you, that is misguided interest in what is best for you and a mother's blind love. Could she see into my heart, she would find there what no Doña Blanca is capable of giving her son. But unfortunately she doesn't know me."

"You're wrong. That's not all of it, nor even the main point. And it's not true that my troubles stem from that marriage."

"If not for Doña Blanca everything would have been different! Tell me, Pedro, what does Doña Blanca look like? They say she's almost a child, and very beautiful. Tell me, is she as beautiful as they claim?"

"No one can compare with you, María, nor do I have eyes for any other woman."

"I know, my darling. But answer me. We women always want to know. Tell me, what does this Doña Blanca look like? Is she tall? Is her complexion fair like her name?* What are her eyes like? Are they light or dark?"

---

*Blanca: white.

"Why talk of her, María? What does that matter to you?"

"Can't you even tell me what the lady looks like, if she's tall or short, if her hair is black?"

"Blond."

"Blond, like yours, then? And her body, Pedro, is that white too?"

"Don't try my patience, woman."

"You're right, forgive me. But don't be cross. I don't want to see clouds on your clear brow, which is the jewel case of my thoughts. I know, my darling, that you can hardly have noticed her. For what man would like to have his bedfellow imposed on him? That alone would make him detest . . . And how could you get along with her? They say she doesn't speak our language."

"I have to go now. Good-bye, María."

"Wait, wait a minute. I have something to say to you. Listen to me, Pedro. I've been thinking that perhaps the queen Doña María may be right, and that her way of loving you is best. She's a mother, and she knows. I have no right to the love of a king, a king as great and as glorious as you, my Pedro. In return for all you've given me, I shall never be able to give you anything more than a love without demands. And if because of that love you had to bear troubles beyond those brought upon you by the Crown, my grief would be endless. I am not of royal blood, though my lineage can compare without dishonor to that of many queens. That's why I want to say this to you: Pedro, think about what's best for you, and if you decide that I'm a hindrance to you, leave me without a moment's hesitation. You've given me the only happiness of my life, and I don't want to be——"

"You say that to me? You? You, too? Woman, don't you know that you're the only thing this embattled king really possesses, the only pillow for his head, the only sentinel for his sleep, the only guardian of his soul, the only treasure of his coffers? Do you think our being apart would lessen the hatred they have for me, the envy that gnaws at me, the violence of brothers who cannot forget their bastardy—so base it makes one doubt whether they are a king's sons? The rage of a mother who could not govern her husband and wants to rule her son? The ambition of vassals who are simply waiting for a chance to steal, and while they tremble in my presence plot treason and make signs to my enemies? Well, if all those evils could be wiped out by my giving you up, I would not give you up. What would all the riches of the world be worth to me without you, María, who are my one true fortune? Leave you? My pursuers would have to besiege this house and stab me with their daggers right here, on this very bed, until the sheets were soaked with my blood, and before I abandoned you my own life would have to abandon me."

"What a joy, dear Pedro, to hear you say those words! Come, nothing will ever separate you from me. Like this, like this, always together, two in one. You'll never leave this embrace, I'll never let you go. I'll never let you embrace that accursed Frenchwoman, my own Pedro!"

If the princess Doña Blanca had not been wronged, how much longer might that muffled war against Don Pedro have dragged on in Castile? The anger of the French king was what, in the end, lent wings to the bastards' rebelliousness, giving shape to their reckless enmity and fair prospects to their blind hate.

Rejected, aggrieved, and insulted, Doña Blanca had finally had to return to her father's court. When, after an arduous journey of many days, she arrived in Paris, she crossed the bridges, entered the palace, and, without speaking to anyone or acknowledging their bows, went right to the chamber where the king was awaiting her. She kneeled down, bowed her head, and kissed his hand. When she had to let it go, she stayed still, in silence, her eyes lowered for the first time since her humiliation. She dreaded meeting again the gaze of those blue eyes she remembered as so gentle and finding them filled with sorrow; finding those lively eyes as she now imagined them to be: hovering full of grief above his daughter's forehead, above her weary eyelids. But when at last she dared confront her father's face, she was frightened to see that his eyes, without the sorrow she expected and feared, were darting furiously, convulsed like salamanders over the flames of his red beard. Then Doña Blanca felt the knot in her throat that had been choking her all the way home grow tighter still. When, with great effort, she managed to control her anguish, a hoarsened voice escaped from her bosom, endlessly repeating one question, one only, at first so stifled as to be nearly unintelligible, then broken with sobs, finally strident in her cries. She asked, "Why, father? Why?" That was all she asked. Her clamor rose until it changed into an inhuman howl. Then she burst into tears. She clawed her face, she tore her hair.

Before such great grief, the king put aside his wrath and opened his arms to his afflicted child that she might flood his neck with tears. Somewhat calmer, but trembling still, Doña Blanca kept asking her despairing question. One would have thought she knew no other word: "Why? Why? Why, father, did you send me there? Tell me, why did you deliver me into their hands like a piece of livestock? Here I am again. I was your daughter. Now I'm nothing more than the testimony of your dishonor. They have spit on your beard, and my presence will remind you of it always. Always!" In vain did he try to persuade her that she would be avenged. And she recoiled at his promise of another marriage, saying, "Never again a horror like that!" and weeping bitterly.

So they had let her rest by herself in her room. And only after a fortnight, spent in semidarkness and grief, could she be brought to confide what she had endured to a lady-in-waiting of her own age. Then she told of the torment of those endless weeks she was forced to spend—as she said—delivered into the hands of appalling lunatics: that Doña María, a withered vine shoot, burning, crackling, her tongue teeming with invectives; those stiff and silent princesses; those gloomy duennas, murmuring through the latrines of their mouths; those men, always involved in endless quarrels, raising their voices to a shout, breaking in on one another, blind, stubborn, oblivious to everything, obsessed with their feuds. And thus, among such people from morning to night, day after day, like one more object of contention, without anyone looking her in her eyes or speaking to her heart. In the last analysis, she explained, the person from whom she had suffered least was Don Pedro, her brutal husband who abandoned her without thinking twice. For why should she have expected any other treatment from him? Was it he who had sought her hand in marriage? She had been delivered to him like a piece of livestock, that was all. Indeed, he had even been too kind to her.

In the meantime, the French king sent emissaries to the bastards of Castile and arranged with them for Don Pedro's destruction: his best warriors would go to fight beside Don Enrique, so that, vanquishing his brother, he himself might wear the royal crown. And that is what happened. Great and glorious armed companies crossed the Pyrenees in support of the count of Trastamara, and they decided the outcome of the war in his favor. There were some, both within the realm and without, who branded Count Enrique's treachery as hideous. Others, justifying him, recalled the beheading of his mother Doña Leonor de Guzmán and the faithless murder of the grand master Don Fadrique, his brother. And the usurper himself,

who allied his spite with that of others, was able to harvest
and sheave many old grudges on behalf of his cause when he
decided to assume the title of King as the banner of his rebellion. He was a man who knew how to make a speech: he chose
his words well; he would tell people what they were hoping to
hear from his lips and, just at the right moment, he would let
something slip from them that no one expected. Thus, when
he was about to undertake the decisive campaign, he assembled his men, and—having described the invincible coalition
of all those who had been injured by the actions of the king
Don Pedro—he reminded each one of his personal grievances,
touched upon their wounds, one after another, and at last
produced the trump card provided by France's help. Was not
the hour come to establish a new reign, prodigal in grace and
fortune? In this way he inflamed hatred, nourished hope,
aroused enthusiasm, stirred ambitions, and fed greed, and his
friends and kinsmen—carried away—exalted him with the
royal purple.

He soon stained his hands that color for the sake of power.
He achieved it by means of violence; and indeed someone,
along the way, had read that bloody destiny in his right hand.
"Yes, you will attain kingly greatness, but at the price, my
lord, of shedding your own blood with this very hand," a
fortune-teller predicted to him three days before the combat
that would deliver the throne to him. It happened when, at
the head of his troop, he was entering a village to spend the
night. With only a small retinue Don Enrique had reached the
town square, where the peasants were enjoying their Sunday
afternoon gathered around some mountebanks, who, on their
way to a fair, were putting on their show of Saracen dances in
the church atrium. The presence of the commander broke up
the festivities. The drum stopped, the shrilling of the cornet
died out in a sour sob, the monkey got away, and a trained

goat—grotesque and astonishing—that was rotating his bulk on a kettle, jumped over the stool with obscene heaviness and fell to the ground. From atop his horse an arrogant Don Enrique faced the peasants' frightened curiosity; and then a little Moorish dancing girl came up to tell his fortune. When the horseman let her take his hand, she promised him a magnificent future after—she said to him—you shed your own blood "with that very hand." He did not care to ask her for an explanation of that ambiguous prophecy. But three days later, when the crucial encounter had been decided in his favor, he saw it inexorably fulfilled.

Once the battle had been won in the fields of Montiel, the Bastard's hosts held the castle in their power, while Don Pedro's were camped outdoors in the dark of the Castilian night, and there, while waiting for dawn, the drama took place. Good intentions, eager for a reconciliation, had arranged a secret meeting between the two kings. In what spirit did each of them go to it? What deceits did they foresee, what fears did they conceal? Perhaps Don Pedro, obedient in adversity to his old tutor, went disposed to compromise, that he might save his crown and buy time at the price of concessions. Perhaps Don Enrique, frightened by his good fortune, was pondering, as he waited for the defeated king in the great hall, surrounded by his best captains, a way to give his usurpation an honest appearance and conceal beneath the terms of a treaty the severity of his military triumph. But when he saw him appear—young, tall, erect, haughty—accompanied by four men only, he felt his courage fail. A great silence greeted Don Pedro's presence.

When at last he reached the center of the hall, he stopped, the only illuminated form in that gathering of shadows. All those around him were quiet. And as that awkward silence continued, they saw the wine of thick pride suddenly rise to the king's face. Red with rage, he raised his voice to ask which among them was the traitor—the infamous, baseborn, bastard count of Trastamára. He ought to have known him by the pallor of his face! On hearing the insult, Don Enrique leaped from his seat and came forward to enact that image evoked in the beginning: with his dagger on high, he advanced on the king. And then both brothers were prisoners, one of the other, in a deadly embrace.

From the threshold, his view cut off at times by the shoulders of the captains who were following the ups and downs of the fight, Don Juan Alfonso watched the contest on which his own life hung. While it lasted, his five senses were attuned to the gasping struggle. But when—their clasped bodies fallen and rolling in the dust—the old servant saw Don Pedro's hand open, and release the dagger, and abandon it on the ground, he turned his back and made his escape. For a while he heard confused shouts pursuing him. "Stop him! After him! After that man!" rang out from afar.

Dialogue of the Dead
A Spanish Elegy

> . . . gnawing worms that from
> within their rotten flesh will eat . . .
> —*The Dance of Death**

Without a lull, hour after hour for many days, it had been raining on the earth. And now the wind was swiftly carrying off the final shreds of clouds, leaving the sky clean, an unlikely blue, while it wrestled muffled screams, and even tears, from the black, mutilated, twisted, desperate, menacing, leafless trees.

There was nothing anywhere. Nothing but silence; a damp silence that oozed, soaking through to the nethermost depths; a silence that was absence and emptiness after the thunderous clash. There was nothing, nothing upon the earth. Beneath it, an infinite number of dead lay buried in confusion, they too almost earth themselves now, and nonetheless still humanity in pain; dead pregnant with the lead of their death; dead contorted in the horror of their martyrdom; dead consumed in the absolute perfection of their hunger; dead. Hastily interred, among the roots of the plants—delivered unto those greedy, insatiable claws now quickened by the rain that had seeped so long in between the rocks and bones.

And the dead, beneath the anguished, seemingly definitive

This dialogue was written in 1939, following the Spanish Civil War.

*An anonymous late fourteenth-century Spanish poem of 79 stanzas. Its theme, widespread in medieval Europe, is that of Death as the great equalizer of all social classes.

muteness of the world, engaged in an underground dialogue, with neither beginning nor end, nor accents, nor pauses. Or perhaps, more exactly, they wove a net of monologues spoken in soft and dampened voices, like the sound of footsteps upon leaves fallen on a path, dirty with mud and with winter.

—This hand—said one—this fistful of bones trying to sink into my empty rib cage, did it belong to a friend or to an enemy? Always there, oppressing my breastbone with a guitarist's cruel ferocity, will I never know what its gesture toward me was in that hour? The uncertainty of that embrace which has become eternal transfers into eternity the anguish of my life, giving it a simple and definitive formula.

And another:

—It's all over now. Now we are all one. The earth unites us. The darkness of the earth makes us equal. It binds us together, as much as our love, our hate. Our common destiny makes us brothers.

—A merciless, mocking destiny if, to make brothers of enemies in the layers of our soil, it destroys everything, stripping it to the bare bone, so that one can no longer tell an embrace from an assault. And not only we, who have hated one another out of love and loved one another out of hate, but also those who came from afar to profane our land with their profiteering greed, only to fall upon thistles and thorns whose cruelty they could not have imagined.

—That's the way it is, however: all equal. And all equal to nothing. To this great and manifest truth lead all the paths of the world.

—In that masquerade of death, who is who, and who knows whom?

—Sunk, forever, in this not knowing.

—Beneath the tread of horses' hooves, beneath the plowshares, beneath the snows, and the suns, and the winds.

—Changed by now into native soil, into the nourishing juice of history, into the pain and pride of those yet living and of those who shall live hereafter.

—But is there still life? Are others still living? Didn't everything stop suddenly one day forever?

—The rivers will still follow their course, clean again after carrying off their heavy, slow spoils (the eyes of their bridges have seen so many, many things!). The seasons of the year will still follow their course in steady rotation. The countryside will flower, and then it will grow severe again. After the violent suns that wrest butterflies of mourning and of fire from the brambles, there will come soft, uncertain suns. But it is scarcely conceivable that other human beings might still be alive beyond our death, behind our backs, nor is it possible to imagine such a life. Could they be the warm blood of our own chilled blood, and could they eat fruits watered with the sap of our hearts? To still be alive! And then what base triviality, what insipid savor would they themselves find in that life, whenever the bitter and glorious aftertaste of the days of sacrifice returned to their mouths! No, a life like that cannot be imagined.

—Nor does it really exist. For they seem like living beings, and perhaps they think they are. But they are only our shadows, bent with pain, silent, wandering, empty, terrified. Many have limbs from their bodies now rotting among us; the souls of all of them are dead. They are projections of ourselves, phantoms, nothing. If they speak, they say nothing. Their voices are confused, they sound like the crystal of goblets shattered by a breeze. One can sense in them the sediment of what was never said and never will be said now. If they laugh, it is with the hollow laughter of a skull, with a laughter of nerves and fright. And their eyes, drawn to the bosom of the earth, are looking for us always; they follow the ants, they try to tell the earthworms from the mire, they seek to send us messages with the animals that burrow in the soil—and they can no longer look straight ahead, they shun one another's gaze. The poor living! What pity their fate deserves! They thought they had escaped with their lives, and life had escaped from them.

—That's not so, for at least they know, they remember. If their lives were cut short like ours, devoid of a future, they in turn have all the past to live over again and savor, and to retrace their paths a thousand times. And they know one another's names, and they can tell who is the enemy. . . .

—And yet, in their shadowy folly, by force of criminal habit, they still murder and are murdered, without hate now, without passion, but listlessly, with reluctance and satiety.

—In all that there must be some sort of life, nonetheless, and even, for a few, some sort of frantic life.

—Then what about the traitors, and the fools, and the sadists (raving lunatics who roamed free), the authors responsible for the tragedy, the executioners, the profound triflers? Some were saved by their obstinacy, others by their inconsistency, the rest by the fatal force of their instinct. Steeled one and all behind their respective insanities, they will live, and live to the full.

—They think they are alive, perhaps, because they're on their feet. But the roots of their being are corrupted.

—Those who perpetrated the treason, blinded by pride and possessed by the rage for power, are protected from the burden of any remorse by the levity of their minds which allows them to accept without question the feeble ideologies (a sarcasm, in the harsh light of today) with which they hastily tried to cover up and give shape to their crime. As for their followers, that deplorable pack of cowards, poor in spirit, cruel out of fear, resentment, and even vulgarity: once their terror has been

sated with terror, they will feel relieved. More grievous will be
the destiny of those in the other band who were responsible.
Of the first, or the last, or the ones most responsible, those
who with their frivolity paved the way for the treason. The
slack, the inhibited, the weak of will, the passive, omissive,
and remiss—now cast into the open air like sad tatters to
ruminate ceaselessly on their guilt. For their hell is made up of
their own clairvoyance, and their torment of their analysis.

—But such is their real life, the one that suits their condition. If the deadly struggle that imprisoned them has finally
come to an end, and they have at last been freed, what more
could they desire? The public positions they had attained with
such effort overwhelmed them. The weight of their coveted
offices and honors came down upon them suddenly, when the
lies in their mouths turned into burning truths. And they
thought they would be crushed and die because their enemies
took so long to come and unbind them. How delightful, now,
to be able to savor the bittersweet of their defeat, far away,
alone! And what secret gratitude they must feel toward their
enemy-liberators who have transformed the unruly populace
into a peaceful populace of corpses! Yes, they too are alive, no
doubt, and alive in their element, like fish in water.

—Just because they were not dead at birth, they are not any
less dead. The will-o'-the-wisp of their intellectualism, of
their professionalism, of their pretenses and their paradoxes
could sometimes pass for the brilliance of life, having never
been more than lying cemetery lights, a charnel-house conceit, and an ossuary ornament.

—Can they make out, in the dense mass of the silence of
the world, in the obstinate hush of the dead and of the mute
shadows that still wander over the surface of the earth, the
veins of scorn toward their being, the green and yellow of
nausea—just as the others no doubt feel flecks of hate spatter-

ing their faces like the hot, livid, acrid spittle of their victims' blood?

—Whatever the case, they all deserve compassion. They too, those of one side and the other. Just because the madman does not see his madness, his raving, be it frantic or sad, he is no less worthy of compassion. For, in reality, in him one pities not so much the man himself as the whole of humanity: its not knowing and not feeling; the pathetic innocence of the new-born; the tottering of old people to whom the world has suddenly grown strange; the desperate groping of everyone toward what they do not understand, or misunderstand. And even, beyond human boundaries, the very wonder of animals subject to a fate they cannot know.

—And must *we* be the ones to pity *them*, who are alive or think they are, the guilty and the traitors? We, the untold legion of the sacrificed, of those who are eating earth and those who must eat—if they are to eat at all—the grass and the roots of the earth?

—Yes, we, who contemplate them from this great, impassive truth, united forever in the anonymity of each one of us and the glory of all.

—We who—the blood still fresh on the lips of the earth, handkerchiefs still damp, the debris still hot, throats worn out, the birds still terrified—have already settled into a severe, impassive, marmoreal, distant immortality.

—But can our terrible death be the foundation for any sort of glory, beyond the pity that rises from the burned and broken stones? Any sort of pride, on top of such great desolation? For, by our doing, beneath the sky, from north to south and from east to west, all geography is a cemetery. A cemetery the marshes, the valleys, the plains, the violent mountains and the gentle estuaries, the orchards and gardens. A cemetery the lagoons and ponds. A cemetery the outskirts of cities, the borders of highways, the beaches, the riverbeds. And men themselves are the cemetery of their dead—they keep their dead, rotting away within them: parents, brothers, children, friends. And enemies. Yes, enemies, for enemies too are carried in the heart, and they make fetid the breath of those who have killed them with their hands or with their wishes.

—The earth has been abandoned, filthy. Starving dogs roam far and wide possessed by their ineffable sadness. They sniff, they follow the tracks of persons who no longer exist, they endlessly chew black rags soiled with mud, and then, exhausted, they stretch out with their muzzles on their paws— sleepless, yearning, hallucinated, crazed, without a master, without a home, without a shadow.

—That is the earth that covers us. And its shores are slowly licked by the oily, heavy sea, thick with salts and iodines, forever vomiting shells, slippery algae, forever threatening to throw up who knows what. The leaden, sluggish, sleeping, mute, insinuating, bitter, ironic sea.

—Perhaps we have rendered sterile the soil for whose love we gave our lives, by sowing it so abundantly with the lime of our bones.

—And if in the hope of remaking our country we have unmade it, if we dreamed of aggrandizing it and the poor bull's hide* has shrunk instead, would the glory of the immense pantheon not be a lie as well? Wouldn't it really be just an immense dunghill, and the bronze and marble memorial no less a fake?

—The anger of destiny cannot outdo itself and make a deplorable chronicle out of the well-won epic of our heroism, of our bottomless resignation and our boundless joy, of our fury and of our hunger, of our firmness and our patience. It

---

*Because of its shape, the map of Spain is frequently compared to a bull's hide.

cannot be so sarcastic as to propose as exemplary what is an example of abnegation and voluntary sacrifice and cheerful surrender and holocaust.

—And yet, after having rolled over valleys and meadows, the thunder of our faith resounds now like a strangely cold peal of laughter. We believed and loved with passion. But after so much fire, all that remains is ashes, soft ashes.

—And the phantoms of our death, of the death of each one, how heavy they are now! The passionate joy of the man who throws his youth into the battle and who, at its liveliest point, bends like a reed, snaps, and falls over broken. The icy courage of the martyr who shoots his scorn like a quivering dart of fine steel at his executioners' eyes—turbid, purulent eyes which only when he is on the ground, and gone, make bold to look at him. The stoicism of one who has managed to keep his dignity in the face of the dishevelled horror of the skies, and has lived a hundred deaths before his limbs were finally scattered among the debris and his throat was smothered in dust. The uncomplaining resignation of one who has felt the needles of hunger eat away his flesh, until surrendering at last, without a word, silent to the end. The desperate anguish of one who has sought out and had to co-erce evasive Death, who was trying to ignore him, and him alone. Is all that remains from this the weight of a bad dream oppressing the heart with its lie? Is it a lie? Are these empty figurations? Is it pure emptiness?

—When the siege is over, the bullfight ended, the sand red with blood, there will remain, at least, vibrating, caught up in the mournful trumpets, the austere emotion of bravery, of bold-ness without malice in the useless struggle against conspiracy.

—The innocent valor of soldiers remains.

—The touching hatred of children.

—The proud grief of women.

—The silent patience of the old.
—Faith without hope.
—Stubbornness without recourse.
—Virtue without praise.
—Duty without recognition and sacrifice without reward.

—All of that remains, indeed. And there it is, made into a symbol, with the fecundity promised to symbolic tragedies. Higher, more essential, because it is futile. Greater and more sacred, because that spirit of such beautiful violence succumbed (strangled by cunning, treacherous powers) beneath hosts of blind forces.

—But all of that is neither mausoleums, nor arches, nor laurels, nor columns, nor gravestones, nor hymns. It is neither marble nor bronze. It is not a pantheon. It is, perhaps, something light, without form, like the gleam of tears in the pupil of an eye, or the pinch of pride and disdain in the silence of a pair of lips. Something like a rose left in a glass of water on the corner of a pine table, or there, within, upon a simple kitchen shelf.

The only thing heard upon the darkened earth was the murmur of a hidden stream.

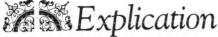# Explication

Written by a Journalist and Archivist at
the Request of the Author, His Friend

This is not the first time that
a writer of established reputation has asked another, less well
known than he, to present a new book to the public. The fact
that the author of this volume, a polygraph whose signature
appears in print with perhaps excessive frequency, turned to
me, an obscure journalist and municipal archivist from the
city of Coimbra, to explain to his readers the meaning of the
work of fiction he offers them here, of course does honor to
our old friendship. But, while demonstrating his confidence in
me, it also reveals a certain lack of confidence in the perspi-
cacity, as well as in the memory, of those presumptive readers,
or else he would not have charged me as my primary mission
to remind them that his first publications—those of Francisco
Ayala, I mean; there, in Spain, almost a quarter of a century
ago—were, like the present one, works of fiction. It is no less
certain, however, that my officious writing would prove unnecessary had he in the meanwhile observed, in his activity as
an author, due respect toward the public. A silence in a
writer's production, however prolonged it might be, is something hardly blameworthy, frequently plausible and deserving
of gratitude; but I do not know to what extent what Ayala has
done—intercalate in those decades a profusion of essays on
political science and even a voluminous *Treatise on Sociology*,

despite his having tempered such arid lucubrations from time to time with studies in literary criticism—could indeed be considered legitimate: it disturbs the image that the public is entitled to form for itself—and even more so nowadays, when specialization prevails—of one whose work it has watched evolve. And it proves vexatious in the extreme that a person who already seemed adequately, definitively, and satisfactorily catalogued as a sociologist should now emerge, shattering once and for all his decorous professorial figure, to which there pertain very specific duties, and present himself again of his own accord, years later, as a writer of fiction.

But he is doing just that, and my job is not to find fault with him, but rather to try and clarify his motives and intentions. Nor, to tell the truth, does this new, or renewed, literary manifestation erupt all that suddenly: one of the narratives that make up the book proceeded, in fact, to sound out public reaction in Buenos Aires a few years ago, and not without success. It had laudatory repercussions; at the time, even one of the leading authorities in Argentine letters, J.L.B.,* judged "The Bewitched" to be "one of the most memorable short stories in Hispanic letters," and he said why. I, for my part, would like to explain the internal features I think I have discovered in *Usurpers,* a book whose diverse pieces make up, in short, a single work having a well-knit unity, as I believe is apparent at first sight.

Its central theme—common to all the tales—is already expressed in the title of the volume in which they are found, and could be formulated in this manner: that power exercised by man over his fellow man is always a usurpation. They all revolve, each within its own orbit, around that terrible,

*Jorge Luis Borges (1899–1986), Argentine poet, critic, and short-story writer.

everyday fact: in "San Juan de Dios," the drive to impose oneself upon and dominate another leads blindly toward self-destruction, the same as in "The Impostors," even if here the eagerness for power is not frustrated by a person's own violence, but rather by virtue of a higher justice. And again in "The Invalid" that frustration comes from the fragility of the support lent to man's imperious desires by his frail constitution. In "The Embrace" those desires are presented to us in the spurt of blood itself: hot, dirty, nauseous. The abjuration of power—inevitable in principle—acquires in "The Bell of Huesca" the character of a mistaken destiny; and—something hinted at in the former albeit in a different way—in "The Bewitched" the same power that in other places is caught gushing forth with the obscene throb of pure life, appears dead, hollow, in the skeleton of an old bureaucratic State.

Evidently, the entire structure of "The Bewitched" (I shall examine it first because, since it is probably known to certain readers, it offers a good initial point of reference), the structure, I repeat, is arranged so as to lead the way through its maze to the vacuum of power. It represents the State, imposing and soulless; in the end it also expresses man's desperate helplessness, the vanity of his earthly labors. I know that the author vacillated, before writing it, in his choice of historical subject, and that he decided in favor of the idiot king after having considered the theme in the form of a mad czar, an interregnum, and a vacant see. His choice of Carlos II, the last degenerate offspring of a most powerful dynasty, seems to me quite a happy one. From the periphery, the alien, obscure, taciturn life of the protagonist tirelessly endeavors to work its way toward the hollow center of the great empire. His point of departure is fresh and natural: Andean summits, his mother, a simple piety. But, as the traveler advances toward the nucleus of royal power, the instances become more and more formalistic, hardened, impenetrable, and humanity grows colder: the supposed narrator is a scholar; the tutor, a friar who is a Latinist; there is a black porter, a crippled beggar, a German confessor, gatekeepers, pages, foreigners, bureaucrats. And, finally—the only woman to appear in the story—a dwarf is the one who introduces him, in return for a bribe, into the sanctuary of majesty, where the imbecile king is found surrounded by diabolical little beasts. A curious ambiguity twinkles in the narrative's title: "The Bewitched" is, without a doubt, Carlos II of Spain; but no less so is the *indio* González Lobo, who strives to reach his presence; and so, too, are the crowds around him. In truth, everyone who pursues power is bewitched, and that could fairly be said of all the other characters inhabiting this book. The pastrycook from Madrigal is bewitched—and let it not be forgotten, his mother appears as a witch: she is brought through the air, wrapped in her widow's cloak. He is formally bewitched upon receiving in the hollow of his hands the pieces of gold with the royal seal. But wasn't the demonic king Don Sebastián, carried away by such mad enterprises, also in turn bewitched? And the Invalid in his bed, and the spying nobles; and the fratricidal sons of King Alfonso; and the irresolute Ramiro; and the Granadan gentlemen, with their mutual hate? But in an analogous manner the title of impostors could be extended to all of them, for legitimate rulers also usurp their power—*non est potestas nisi a Deo**—and must bear it as a burden of guilt. And so, too, can all of them be deemed sickly, for they all suffer from the weakness common to the human condition.

Thus, the six tales, animated by such a deep unity of mean-

---

*"There is no power but of God" (Rom. 13:1).

ing, interrelate in different ways, linking and modulating their respective themes. They can be shuffled, ordered, and regrouped, like a hand of cards. The principal intuition of "The Bewitched" has already been noted: the State, as a structure of empty power. That intuition is also found in "The Bell of Huesca," where an astonishing testament has left the vacant throne in the trust of the military Orders, and where the scepter passes into the hands of a prince who covets it not. Nor is the Invalid capable of exercising royal power in Castile. And the Portuguese realm has fallen captive with the loss of Don Sebastián. Something similar happens in the Moorish realm of Granada, whose noble lineages prolong the discord that has crushed it. On the whole, the idea of an organization of power, emptied of the life that built it, poses a significant contrast to the elemental violence of "The Embrace," where the emotions of kinsfolk driven by ambition, jealousy, resentment—in short, by the crudest passions—are all intermixed. This story of fratricide was first going to be called "The Brothers" and, according to my understanding, without a shadow of irony: it presents the natural sources of discord, so blended in the blood with love, and of the drive to dominate, that is, the opposite pole to the juridical and bureaucratic order of the State. But the same idea is also found in the other tales. Not only in "San Juan de Dios"—which, in turn, could also have been called "The Brothers," and I think it would have been a better title, for there it is a question at the same time of blood brothers and the brothers of the Institute of San Juan de Dios; not only in "The Invalid" whose protagonist with his physical infirmity envies the strength of his mentally infirm foster brother, but in "The Bell of Huesca" as well, where the undaunted primogeniture of one prince has disheartened the other, who strives even after death to incapacitate him (his brother here transforms resentful hate into renunciation); and also in "The Bewitched," which has the postulant set out on a trip to the Court, moved by his nostalgia for a powerful and unknown father. And it is important to note that the author does not inexorably confine those human beings undergoing the experience of power between the extremes of cold and soulless organization on the one hand and the elemental movements of the spirit on the other. If the abjuration of the world is in "The Bell of Huesca" mere laxity and false piety, in "San Juan de Dios" it is ardent charity. In this way the tales, which aspire as a whole to be exemplary, leave a pious course partly open for human nature to save itself from desperation.

With this, the ideological elements visible at first sight in *Usurpers* have been briefly described. The excesses of our era and the author's personal experiences justify his perceiving and underscoring what is demonic, deceptive, and vain in the eagerness to dominate, and his view that the health of the spirit resides in saintly resignation.

Why, however, does he appeal to the conscience of his readers, not from the common ground of those immediate experiences shared, more or less closely, by all our generation, but through "examples" far removed in time? Probably, in order to extract from them their essential meaning, which is obscured, when one operates on the basis of current circumstances, by inevitable partisan bias.

But by proceeding in this way, he exposes himself to the well-known risks of the historical genre, which, despite incessant offshoots, has already had its season of maturity and bears the stigma of a subsequent decadence, prodigal in watery and insipid fruits. He could not have been unaware of these risks, since the materials he utilizes were exploited before him by poets, dramatists, and novelists—writers sometimes less than middling—of Spanish Romanticism and post-Romanticism:

after the ballads of the Duque de Rivas,[*] King Pedro's deeds, preserved in the austere prose of Chancellor López de Ayala,[†] stirred the frondage of the feuilletonist Fernández y González,[‡] who also popularized the pastrycook from Madrigal, an unconfessed traitor and martyr for Zorrilla[§]; and even the politician Cánovas del Castillo[‖] permitted himself a novel about the uncertain legend of Don Ramiro the Monk. If the author decided now to rework these materials, already handled by so many, it is perhaps because he found in them the advantage of historical situations that are well known but nevertheless, because of their remoteness, without the weight of interests borne by those of our living experience, and consequently more capable of rendering the essential intuitions pursued by him through his new artistic treatment. It is hardly necessary to point out that these narratives at best cull only the crux of each respective situation insofar as it seems significant for the author's esthetic intentions; the characters are either entirely imaginary—the active characters of "San Juan de Dios" and

---

[*]Angel Saavedra, duque de Rivas (1791–1865), Spanish Romantic poet and dramatist. Two of his well-known *Historical Ballads* treat episodes from the life of Pedro I: "The Alcazar of Seville" describes the king's assassination of his half-brother, the grand master Don Fadrique, while in "The Fratricide" Pedro is himself killed by another half-brother, Don Enrique de Trastamara.

[†]Pedro López de Ayala (1332–1407), chancellor of Castile, statesman, poet, and the first important modern historian of Spain. His *Chronicle of the King Don Pedro* is a vivid, intensely dramatic history of the reign of Pedro I.

[‡]Manuel Fernández y González (1821–88), popular and prolific Spanish writer of serialized novels. A number of his historical novels take place during the reign of Pedro I. He also wrote *The Pastrycook from Madrigal*.

[§]José Zorrilla (1817–93), the most representative, and famous, poet and dramatist of Spanish Romanticism. His play *Traitor, Unconfessed, and Martyr* offers a version of the story of the supposed impostor Gabriel Espinosa.

[‖]Antonio Cánovas del Castillo (1828–97), Spanish conservative politician, historian, and man of letters; author of a historical novel, *The Bell of Huesca*.

"The Bewitched" lack any historical basis whatsoever; the saint and the king have here only a very slight one—or else they have been drawn in the freest manner, according to those same intentions. The period atmosphere is reduced to summary indications: there is not a single archeological recon- struction in the entire book; it never succumbs to the facile and false novelesque charm that, by escaping to past times, usually turns into a masquerade. A few succinct notes suffice to situate the action, giving it a precise reference—occasion- ally, a date—that acts as a retaining wall against timeless fantasy, which is also weak. Thus, the reader's attention, drawn toward the period in question, is not obliged to give in to its fancy wardrobe.

However, the setting of an action in historical time makes certain demands, one of them being linguistic accommoda- tion—in which the author runs the risk of slipping into pas- tiche, of performing idiomatic archeology. The device fre- quently used by some modern writers in order to avoid this is to give the treatment of their materials—oftentimes expurgated with notable scholarly effort—an ironic slant, or else to season them with humorous anachronisms. A subtle or burlesque wink to the reader, which responds not so much to an internal need of the work as to the need experienced by the person writing it to safeguard himself against any suspicion of pedantry or of innocent Romanticism, and which, though binding the work to the present, does so in a way both artificial and external, even if not devoid of merit. The author of this book has dis- dained such a safe device; he has preferred, without disguising his own spontaneous style, to give each narrative a restrained period inflection, which suggests but does not imitate; and, of course, he has avoided the introduction of dictionary archa- isms. Thus, for example, the agitated, pathetic atmosphere of "San Juan de Dios" is reflected in a certain verbal emphasis, especially in the speeches uttered by both of the gentleman, in order to trace, directly and dramatically, the story of their rivalry and of their impassioned struggle. Equally emphatic is the way in which, during its course, the signs of destiny appear—the punishment of violent hands, amputated by steel; that of lascivious hands, forced to touch, in death, the flesh whose warmth they had profaned—among the many such contrasts offered by the story. But this elevated tone is highlighted against a twofold background of the boy's simple and sometimes brutal naturalness and the saint's dark, pious effusiveness, not free from an occasional touch of peasant shrewdness. Furthermore, the presentation of the entire plot, beginning with an old painting, conveniently distances the narration and frames it. And if from here we move on to "The Bewitched," we shall find, on the contrary, a language whose sobriety borders on poverty: feelings must remain hidden, suppressed; it is devoid of all verbal splendor of the sort displayed at times in "The Impostors"—there especially—where baroque language cloaks by casting in preestablished forms both the impulses of runaway ambition and a tender, maidenly love, obliged to declare itself through ornamental formulae imposed by a high culture. What more could be said? The reader will see without anyone else's help how the internal requirements of each narrative have determined the technique of its literary development: the vague air of a chronicle in "The Bell of Huesca"; scholarly composure in "The Bewitched"; an extremely varied rhythm, from majesty to mockery, in "The Impostors"; the changes of perspective in "The Invalid," where one passes from the monologue of the helpless sick man to the chatter of his lowly servants, only to return again to the frustrated exemplary lesson ordered by the king; he will note that if the latter's weakened constitution prevents him from commanding respect, the same effect will be produced in the bishop by his own exuberant constitution; he will observe in "The Embrace" the barbarous play of visceral passions as seen through the astute, clear-sighted eye of a courtier and partisan, incapable, despite his ability and good sense, of channeling events in a reasonable way; and perhaps when he sees him recall certain very intimate scenes of the king with his mistress, the reader will ask himself how the old favorite could possibly have known them in such detail. . . .

I consider the task entrusted to me done. It consisted of explaining, at the author's request, the latent intentions of his book, not of judging to what extent he has been able to realize them in an artistic form: our exceedingly close friendship renders me unfit to do that. Let the reader, then, on his own account and at his own risk, be the one to judge.

F. de Paula A. G. Duarte
Coimbra, Spring 1948